The Black Moon

David Brookes

The Black Moon

SeaCrab Books

SeaCrab Books

This edition published

0800 GMT on

15th May 2023

© David Brookes 2023

David Brookes asserts the moral right
to be identified as the author of this work

ISBN: 9798394749919

Dedicated

to YOU,

the Reader,

without whom this book would serve no purpose.

G10 Advanced Notification Infrastructure
activated...Emergency procedures initiated...
breach imminent...evacuation of leadership
priority... experimental subjects expendable...

auto-destruct measures on Standby...

Chapter 1

"Shelton!"

"Shelton!"

I became aware that somebody was shouting the word 'Shelton'. I opened my eyes. A soldier wearing a full-faced helmet was struggling to keep the door closed against the pressure of something which was trying to gain entry.

A woman dressed like a nurse was pulling at my arm, trying to get me to stand up and out of bed. She was the one calling out the name Shelton – and she was addressing me while she did it.

"You need to come with me Mister Shelton - and damned quick if you value your skin!" I wasn't sure if I did value my skin, but acquiesced to her urgent request. I was wearing green and white striped pyjamas.

"Quick – get your slippers on and shift your arse!" I allowed her to place the slippers on my feet and drag me through a door on the other side of the small room from where the soldier was losing his battle to keep his door shut. I caught a glimpse of random arms and legs – no doubt belonging to the people trying to get in.

I sensed that I was in grave danger and began to run in the direction the nurse was leading me. As we turned into a long dark corridor, I heard shouting and gunfire coming from the room we had just left.

We entered a small foyer – a hospital foyer. The nurse turned toward the main exit, beckoned for me to hurry. I hurried. I could hear people coming down the corridor behind us and I didn't like the sound of them.

Parked outside was a large black car with the rear door open. As we approached, a man leaned out of the front passenger window and said "Get in, quick!" We got in, quick. The nurse slammed the door and shouted "Go!, Go!"

As the car raced away at high speed, the man in the front fired his gun at our pursuers, who decided they didn't want to get shot and went back inside the building.

The car moved at high speed through city streets – I had no idea what city it was. I was having trouble knowing anything. I seemed to have lost my memory – all I knew was that a nurse had helped me escape from some people who wanted to harm me for some reason. Now a man in dark glasses and another wearing a chauffeur's uniform were driving me through an unknown city at high speed.

"I don't suppose anyone would like to tell me what's going on?" I enquired in a voice which sounded like it hadn't been used for a long time.

"Don't worry, Mr. Shelton, we are nearly there – all will be explained soon. You've lost your memory but it is only temporary" said the nurse in her best comforting nurse voice. I did feel calmer too. I relaxed a little, silently observed the buildings we passed by – office blocks, shopping centres, the usual. The normality soothed my nerves – though I had no idea what my nerves had to be nervous about.

Ten minutes later, the car pulled into a small side street, before turning right, moving down a ramp which led to an underground car park. At the far end of the car park, we stopped at a barrier, guarded by three uniformed policemen, carrying machine guns.

The driver wound down his window, mumbled something to the guard. He must have liked it because he opened the barrier and let us through into another smaller car park, which in turn led to a dark ramp.

We went down to a lower car park. The driver pulled into a bay at the far end – beside some reinforced doors, also guarded.

"OK Mr Shelton, we have arrived – you will soon be able to rest and recuperate" said the nurse.

"Thanks" was all I could think of to say – so I said it. The nurse laughed.

"There's no need for you to thank us Sir, it is you who deserve thanks" I looked blank – and felt blank too - but let it go at that – either I would find out what was going on or I wouldn't – it didn't seem to matter all that much to me one way or the other.

The nurse held my arm in a supportive gesture as we went inside the secured building. Corridors, corridors, corridors – and then double doors into a large, well appointed bedroom with all the trimmings – a room fit for a tired member of the aristocracy. I didn't complain – just let them put me to bed and tuck me in. The nurse smiled as she fussed over me – her smile cheered me inside, made me feel safe.

"What's your name Nurse?" I enquired.

"Susan" she replied, smiling once more.

"Nice to meet you Susan, I'm... can't remember at the moment, sorry"

"You're Mr. Shelton, Sir... the Prime Minister"

Chapter 2

They spent the next few days telling me things. They told me I was Michael Shelton – Prime Minister of The United Kingdom. They told me I had lost my memory. They told me I had been kidnapped and brainwashed by some sort of rebel group, that I was now safe and back where I belonged. They told me it would take a few weeks to get me back to work, running the country at a time of severe crisis. They told me I had been 'missing' for several months, that they had recently located me and brought me back.

I was not allowed any newspapers. They informed me I would need to acclimatise slowly to certain things which had happened to the country – and the world in general. They told me these events were of a tragic nature, that I would be enlightened incrementally so as not to overload my brain – which itself had undergone severe trauma due to advanced psychological techniques and activities which the rebels had forced me to undergo.

Nothing they told me made the slightest bit of sense. I didn't believe any of it. I just let them talk, nodded my head when I deemed it appropriate. This went on for several days.

Then they told me that there had been a nuclear explosion which had destroyed a large part of south east England. The rebels had done it about a year ago. I wasn't told why, or who they were. I didn't care in the least.

When they weren't telling me things, they were sedating me 'for my own good' as I needed to rest - my brain and nervous system required peace and quiet to compensate for the shock it had experienced.

I enjoyed the sleeping part best. The food was good too. Nurse Susan was attractive and kind. That was enough for me.

Then a man started coming in to ask me questions and ruined it all. No matter how many questions I answered – or tried to answer – he always had more. He asked me about people whose names meant nothing to me – places I had never been... on and on. I did not like this man.

He never told me his name – only questioned me for about 30 minutes every day. He asked me about a man named Michael Garvie and a man named Johnny Walsh and a man named Mark Hopkins. I knew nothing of these people and told him so. He did not seem pleased with my answers. That was fine by me because I was not pleased with his questions.

After a few weeks, this man stopped coming. I was let out of bed, given the run of a nicely appointed apartment. I saw Nurse Susan every day – she brought me food, took my blood pressure, smiled at me. I began to feel more like myself again – though I had no idea who I actually was. Nurse Susan always called me 'Prime Minister' or Mr. Shelton. I began to wonder if it were possible that I was indeed the Prime Minister, Mr. Shelton. I certainly lived in the type of surroundings I imagined a Prime Minister would inhabit.

I had no plans. I would need to know who I was to know what sort of plans to make. If I was really Prime Minister Shelton, I would need to hold briefings with my cabinet. Nobody purporting to be from any cabinet came to see me. There wasn't the merest hint of a Personal Private Secretary or a Minister for Health.

I began to complain to everyone I came into contact with. In turn everybody told me I would be fine and not to worry, my memory would come back soon. They didn't believe it any more than I did. Maybe I would never find out the secret to my true identity. I didn't care any more.

I simply wanted to get away from this luxury prison. I had been denied the right to leave the apartment – to go outside for a walk, read newspapers or watch television. My only reality was the one they allowed me – and that didn't seem very convincing.

I started planning my escape – *from* what and *to* what I had no clue, but I felt I'd go completely off my trolley if I stayed here much longer. My desire to get away and to make my own decisions, became stronger with each stifling, tedious day. I needed freedom at any cost – and I was determined to get it.

I was awoken early next morning by Nurse Susan, who told me that I was to be transferred to another 'facility'.

"Facility?" I quipped "Sounds delightful".

Nurse Susan grimaced, then laughed "Probably a car park or oil refinery they've got hidden away somewhere". Her use of the terms 'they' and 'hidden' indicated to me that perhaps she also had misgivings, suspicions concerning her employers. I decided to press her for information.

9

"Sounds like you're no fan of your bosses – have you worked for them long?"

"I was transferred to this department from the military hospital I worked in before. Didn't exactly volunteer"

"Not enjoying your new job then?"

"If I'm honest, no. I understand that it's all part of the security strategy – whatever that is, but I'd rather be tending injured soldiers" - She stopped short as she considered that maybe she had offended me.

"Rather than mad old bastards who can't remember what day it is?" I laughed and she joined in. "I quite understand what you mean Nurse" I said.

"It's not you", she laughed again. "It's the cloak and dagger mystery of it all. I don't even know who it is I'm actually working for – just that it's some government department"

"And I'm not the Prime Minister!" I said it in such a way as to shock her into reacting before she could control herself. The look on her face was priceless. She nodded in agreement before forcing her features into a blank expression. Then a look of deep sadness washed fleetingly across her visage. It looked like two sides of her mind were fighting for control.

"OK, you got me. It's true" she looked around as if frightened of cameras or recording equipment which might be monitoring us. "Whatever you do, don't let them know you know that – you'd become worthless to them if you said anything".

I was relieved to get an honest answer from somebody at last but a little shocked to hear my suspicions confirmed. I had never believed that I was the Prime Minister but could not think of a reason why anyone would want to convince me that I was. Also it had been something on which I could base the tiny sense of identity I still had. A fake identity is better than zero identity. Now I had nothing. Nothing factual. I had only feelings and instincts to guide me. It had been a feeling of weird disbelief which had led me to conclude that what I was being told was a lie.

"Why though?" I didn't expect an answer, was really just thinking aloud.

"Have you heard of Black Moon?" she asked – a look of fear accompanied by shifting, cautious eyes.

"Nope"

"G10?"

"No – hang on there a minute, rings a tiny far away little bell, that does"

"That's good. You've been involved with that organisation for several years so there must be some residual memory which could be activated"

"You sound like a machine, talking like that"

"Sorry, I guess I've been involved with G10 too long myself"

"In what capacity?"

"What do you think?" she sounded a bit miffed at my comment. Maybe she thought I suspected her of being more than a nurse. In which case she would be right. I couldn't remember much but I had feelings and they told me to trust absolutely nobody – especially if they started acting like they were on my side.

"Hard to tell these days".

"I take your point" she laughed

"Is there any way I can get out of this ponced up prison?" I was always straight to the point – you got a more truthful reaction that way. I was surprised by *her* lack of surprise. Her face reassembled itself – was she thinking of letting me into a secret, considering taking me into her confidence?

"Look, I would like to help you but – well it's a lot easier said than done".

"I can believe that – will you help me get out of here? – after all you are partly responsible for my being here in the first place – remember – the daring escape with the shooting and the quick getaway. I don't know when or where – or why – it happened but I do remember that it did".

"So, your memory of more recent events is intact, I see. That's a good sign"

"Never mind all that – can you get me out of here?"

She became serious. "Look, as I told you earlier – you are being moved to a new facility later today. If I can contact some friends of mine in time, it might just be possible to get you away – but why do you want to escape? – you don't know who you are – who anyone else is, or what's going on – that won't change just because you're in a new location will it?"

"You've got a point but I have learned to follow my instincts – facts have a tendency to be unreliable in my experience".

"That's true enough in your case" She stood up and turned towards the door. "Just leave it with me – if there's anything I can do, I will set it up – but I cannot promise anything I'm afraid"

"Just one thing Susan" she turned to look at me. "Do you know who I really am?"

"I know who you were – before the Stacking began" she looked sad now – no doubt aware of some terrible things which had happened to me – things which I was perhaps lucky not to know.

"Well?" I snapped – I was getting fed up with talking in circles.

"You started out as a man named Michael Garvie"

Chapter 3

After Susan had gone - hopefully to get in touch with some people who could extricate me from my current situation, I tried to get some sleep. I was partially successful in this endeavour, although my mind was awash with vague images of people and places I felt I knew but which I could put no names to, nor combine into an acceptable narrative. Perhaps it was a sign that my memory was at last attempting to reassert itself.

A doctor entered, took my blood pressure and various other medical data – possibly to ensure that it was safe to transport me to wherever it was that some faceless, nameless people wanted to place me.

Nurse Susan was conspicuous by her absence. I worried that she had got herself arrested or worse for her candid talk earlier – surely this room was bugged and monitored – I had no way of knowing but felt it unlikely that people who seemed to want absolute control over me would allow for the possibility of plots and plans being made against them in secret.

It was getting dark when the doctor returned, accompanied by two armed soldiers and a man I had never seen before, wearing a double-breasted blue pinstripe suit and a bowler hat – some sort of caricature of a 1960's London stockbroker. He didn't introduce himself and seemed to be running the show – barking orders to the military men and asking me if I would be good enough to accompany him.

"Where we going?" I enquired "A day out at the seaside perhaps?"

"You wish" was all he said in reply.

I meekly followed orders, walked behind 'The Stockbroker' and the doctor – the armed guards close behind – we passed along a circuitous maze of faceless corridors, stairwells and double doors until we arrived at a lift. The indicator light told me we were on floor 12 – this meant absolutely nothing to me. I began to wonder if the new facility I was to be taken to was close by, possibly connected by corridors or tunnels – in which case I would not go outside at all – making the chances of anyone rescuing me somewhat less than I had hoped.

I was pleased when we went down in the lift to the ground floor and into a wide foyer. Outside I saw a big black car waiting.

We crossed the atrium, stepped outside into a light drizzle. The feeling of cool natural breeze and little misty droplets on my face felt amazing. I realised that I needed to be outside, away from these anonymous dry people.

"Please get into the back of the limousine" said The Stockbroker. I made to comply. It was then that all hell broke loose – to use an over-utilised cliché.

Somebody pushed me to the ground. A loud explosion occurred. Bits of debris fell onto me – my left arm took a powerful impact. Machine guns began firing. Shouting was heard.

I closed my eyes as the excruciating pain in my arm hit home. I was dragged onto my feet, along the pavement. A man's voice behind me

15

shouted "Get in the fucking car!" I was pushed into a vehicle. The vehicle sped off.

Some bullets smashed through the rear window, raked the interior of the vehicle with hot lead. A man beside me in the back of the car, fell onto me and lay still. I opened my eyes – a bleeding corpse, eyes staring blankly, lay across me. I shoved it away, it fell against the inside of the car door.

The vehicle jammed on its brakes. Something hit us from behind, jarring my neck painfully. We then accelerated away, swerved around corners. The corpse fell on me again. I pushed it off once more.

The vehicle slowed a little, we continued in a straight line. I opened my eyes again. We were in a city – a main thoroughfare with several lanes of traffic. I noticed that the driver of the vehicle was a young man wearing black military combat gear.

"Relax Mr. Garvie – we'll soon have you back to reality" he laughed to himself as he said this. Some private joke no doubt. My arm hurt and I didn't like it. I closed my eyes and grimaced in pain for a bit.

Next time I looked, we were travelling more slowly through countryside.

"Welcome back – soon be somewhere safe where we can get that arm looked at – you took a couple of bullets in it". I didn't bother replying – couldn't think of an appropriate response.

Then I said "Where's Nurse Susan?" The driver looked a little puzzled at first – maybe he didn't know who I was talking about. Then he smiled to himself and said "Back at work". That was it.

We pulled into a narrow lane, turned left into what looked to me like a military barracks. After passing though a couple of checkpoints, the car pulled up outside a low building with a sign stating that it was Block 'C'.

A soldier opened the passenger door, dragged the dead man away. I clambered weakly out, stood gazing into the distance – which was mainly fields. I had not seen any distance for a long time and it felt good to be in an open space – close to nature.

My reverie was cut short however by another soldier who took my right arm and began leading me into the building.

"Better get that arm seen to sir – it's looking nasty". I shrugged, let him half-drag me into the foyer. I wanted to make a funny remark but couldn't think of one.

Chapter 4

I was back in bed again – though this time I had a window and was allowed to come and go if I felt like it. I was no longer sedated either – I could visit the toilet or have a shower without asking anyone. This in itself – while nothing to write home about under normal circumstances – was a big deal to me. I was being treated like a free human being again. I could select my preferred meals from a daily menu and the doctor I saw explained that I was being kept in a low-stress environment in order to give my arm time to heal after the recent surgery I had undergone to remove two bullets – I also required time for my mind to become calm, which would, they hoped allow my memories to slowly return.

They told me little about what had been happening but informed me it was only because they didn't want to stir up my confusion again. This I believed because an officer had visited me when I first arrived here and had informed me that at an appropriate time they would give me a full debrief concerning the incidents and events which had overwhelmed me – they would clarify - put things in perspective for me. This would get me back to as normal as I was likely to get in the short term.

I accepted everything I was told without question – mainly because I could think of no questions – and because I had nothing else to believe whatsoever – my mind was pretty blank. I quite liked it that way. I needed rest, enjoyed the peace and quiet. Questions could come later.

Nurse Susan was nowhere to be seen. When I asked about her I was told she was back at work – she was doing a very good job, rescuing 'people like me' who had undergone 'intense psychological warfare processing' and was not likely to appear on my radar for the foreseeable future. I was reassured that she was safe. I hoped that one day I might be able to thank her personally for what she had done for me. I might also see her radiant smile again.

I spent a week just lazing around, eating decent food and reading pulp novels – I was kept away from newspapers as reading them might upset my mental equilibrium if subjected to negative news stories. A positive, peaceful, healthy environment was required. I was happy to go along with that. For now at least.

As the weeks passed, I became calmer, a little bored. My memory started to show small signs of re-engagement. For instance, I was beginning to remember that I was in fact Michael Garvie – though no memories of actual events appeared to back up this growing conviction. The doctor – as well as the military staff - were under orders to always address me as Michael and it began to feel right. I suppose if they had all consistently addressed me as Jeremy or George – I would have got used to that as well – but I certainly felt comfortable as Michael.

I was shown a copy of a birth certificate proving that a man – purported to be me – was born to parents on a certain date and was brought up in a small town. This same Michael Garvie was seen to have joined the navy after leaving school and to have bought a house in Winchester some years later. Not much of this rang any bells for me though, and I paid little more than a cursory interest.

It was the little boat – named 'Beach Boy' which first clicked into place as a certainty. I was shown some photographs of the small marine craft and warm feelings were generated. I was informed that this was my own boat and that it was moored in Dover in a large marina. I asked if I might be allowed to go to see this boat. They told me I could not only go to see her but take her out on the water if I wanted to – I would be accompanied by a couple of the camp guards just to be on the safe side. I was fine with that as there were obviously hostile forces involved in my situation and I had no confidence in my ability to cope with anything untoward.

The next morning I climbed into the rear seat of a rather luxurious large black saloon car and was joined by two tough looking soldiers – rather uncomfortable in civilian clothes – and a driver who wore a military uniform and beret.

It was a long drive – apparently the base I was living on was near Hereford – to the far west of England, and Dover – where my boat was moored was situated to the far east of the country. These place names and concepts of distance meant nothing to me at all.

It took about seven hours to reach Dover. I found it fascinating to look out of the window, see the passing countryside, the towns we travelled through and the stops we made at service stations. I had not seen more than a handful of people for as long as I could remember – which was not very long – and started to feel less alone as a consequence. I began wondering just who this Michael Garvie – who I myself – was. I hoped it was true that I owned a boat as the idea of pottering about in water appealed to me.

We pulled up next to a jetty and climbed out of the car. Moored close by was a 24ft *Finesse* craft painted blue and white. I recognised the boat instantly and this shock of recognition made me physically stumble and almost fall.

"You OK Mr. Garvie?" asked one of the guards – a tall blond brute named Simon, wearing a tan brown polo neck jumper.

"Yeah, yeah, I'm alright – just surprised myself by recognising the boat. I know it – it is my boat!" I almost shouted in my excitement. The two guards smiled at each other.

"Let's get on board" suggested the other guard – a dark complexioned man named Charles, wearing a black overcoat. By his general demeanour and the fact that he had been sitting in the front passenger seat of the car on the way down here, I surmised him to be the higher ranking of the two men.

We wasted no time moving down the jetty and onto the deck of my boat. I sat on the gunwale and felt the gentle rocking of the craft in the water. It felt good. I knew then that I was indeed Michael Garvie and that I owned a boat named '*Beach Boy*'.

"If you want to go out onto the water for a short trip, that's fine – can you remember how to start her up?"

"Of course I can!" I felt slightly offended that this guy thought I was too dumb to start my own boat. I stomped to the cockpit and fired the diesel engines into life. Simon and Charles looked surprised but pleased.

"Somebody untie us then!" I commanded. Simon did so and gripped on tight as I powered the boat forward with no warning. The sense of power – albeit not that great - was marvellous – the fact that I was controlling anything and was free to move though open water at will quickly rejuvenated my long crushed spirit. I spent a good half hour whizzing up and down – turning tightly – slowing – accelerating - thoroughly enjoying myself. I then slowed the boat to a stop and went below to have a look around. It seemed somewhat familiar – like when you get home after a long holiday and your house seems a bit different to how you remember it – although you recognise it as your house. This is how I felt now.

I found a bottle of Captain Morgan's Spiced Rum in a cupboard and poured myself a glass. The liquid burned my throat, felt hot in my stomach. It lifted my spirits to a new level – it was the memory which lifted me – even more than the alcohol. I knew beyond doubt that what I had been told since arriving in the camp in Hereford was true. Michael Garvie was back!

Chapter 5

I spent the next few days at the military camp near Hereford. I was no longer content to stay in my room or receive so many medical visits. As my mind slowly began to reassert itself, I was given snippets of information – not too many too quickly – for fear of unsettling my nervous system.

I was informed by a Captain Hughes, that I had been the subject of some advanced psychological brainwashing techniques, the aim of which had been to attempt to turn me into a mindless zombie who could be programmed by certain people at will. I was not alone in this. There were in fact hundreds of people in varying degrees of processing, some beyond hope of recovery.

I had been a borderline case and it was thought I was beyond saving for a long time. It seemed my boat had rescued me. My memories of *Beach Boy* had been deeply embedded in my psyche. The pleasant associations had not been erased by the brainwashing and still lurked deep inside my subconscious. There was now some hope that more of my memories of who I had been before the processing had started, could be salvaged.

I was given a file with the word IPCRESS on the front cover. This was supposed to clarify and explain at least some of the theories and applications relating to the psychological techniques which had been used on me over an extended period.

The language was technical and extensive. I understood little, but enough to realise that I had been part of a project which had begun way back in the cold war era of the 1960s. The organisation behind the IPCRESS process had been almost completely blown apart when a renegade agent of the British Secret Service had broken his programming and shot the double agent behind the early programming operation.

Unfortunately the process was still known - had slowly been improved and adapted over the years. The organisation behind it grew and changed it's name to G10. It was so successful that it deeply infiltrated MI5 and MI6 as well as parts of the British Constabulary. G10 were now a powerful and dangerous organisation, a major threat to global stability.

I had been in the clutches of these people for a number of years, had become their plaything. They had programmed me to do their bidding, to believe almost anything they wanted me to believe. It was even stated that at one point – just before my initial – 'false rescue' – whatever that meant, they had convinced me I was living on the moon, fighting evil aliens. I found this extremely hard to credit - I had no memories relating to these mental manipulations – the doctors informed me that my mind had taken itself offline in an effort to avoid complete disintegration of my will and personality.

G10 had gone too far with me – I had almost been rendered useless after they convinced me that several nuclear bombs had gone off and that I was somehow involved in this. It was then that they had staged a false rescue – when I first met Nurse Susan. I was relieved to be told that she was a deep cover agent, pretending to be a member of G10. She had been obliged to take part in the fake rescue to keep her cover intact. She had hoped that the new location would be a little easier to extricate me from – which it did eventually turn out to be when I was being transferred to yet another location. Susan was now back inside the G10 operation – gathering information on their activities when she could and rescuing their victims when possible. I had been one such rescued subject.

The concept of a 'false rescue' was typical of the way G10 operated. They added layer upon layer of chaos and confusion, which increased the subject's sense of vulnerability. A vulnerable person – out of their depth, confused and fearful - is perfect ground for the planting of ideas and beliefs which may serve the purposes of G10 – to the detriment of their victim and any targeted person.

One of the main goals of the G10 treatment was to create hidden assassins who didn't know they had been programmed – upon specific keywords, images sounds, or other locked-in stimuli – to kill specified targets. I was told they had been successful in placing these programmed killers in several high positions within the British Secret Service. Several had been discovered but it was thought there were many more of these time-bombs waiting to go off at their appointed time.

I was being prepared for a hit-job on a man named Shelton – a man who I had been told I was and who I had been informed was the British Prime Minister. It sounded crazy but confusion and stress were the main ingredients of their programming methods and rendered their victims completely open to any suggestions or manipulations.

A person who is on the edge of insanity because his sense of identity has been partially erased, is desperate to cling to any consistent concept as the truth. It was stability and consistency he sought above all else – it mattered not if the beliefs he was consistently subjected to by those who brainwashed him were true or false – the very concept of truth was blurred so much in his mind as to become an irrelevance – it was safety and psychological wholeness at any cost which he sought.

Once certain ideas – and the necessity of certain actions - had been deeply rooted in his psyche – a man would happily think and act in any way which supported those ideas. It didn't have to make sense – it just had to be consistent, something his mind could cling to in order to pacify itself and minimise the horrible sense of madness the IPCRESS programming had instilled.

They had worked on me hard – eventually convincing me that nuclear bombs had gone off and that I was fighting evil aliens.

When Captain Hughes first informed me of these facts, I laughed incredulously. It was nonsense.

As time passed, however, I gradually became aware of an unsettling memory of a nuclear bomb having actually gone off – it felt like a truth which I had repressed, which I now began to remember. It didn't feel like a lie. It felt true. Obviously even now I was not free of the programming – far from it – I was at a stage where I was only beginning to recover the memories of these things – the feelings

I experienced were not that I had been brainwashed but that these things were true – even though I had evidence that they were not true – after all I was in England and there was no nuclear winter. My mind believed it had actually happened, whilst simultaneously observing that the belief was untrue – it was not a nice feeling at all.

My doctor gave me a mild sedative after some of these terrible revelations had been made to me – it was important that my mind not be overloaded at this crucial stage – it was possible I could click back into the programmed belief system if I was pushed too hard.

I spent a long time – many months - slowly becoming clearer as to my actual situation and the events which had led up to it.

It was only after I had to a large degree, absorbed and come to terms with the most outlandish and bizarre ideas that G10 had programmed me to believe and experience that Captain Hughes – and another army type who introduced himself as Lieutenant Smith – began revealing to me the brainwashing I had received concerning my more personal affairs.

They began by asking me if I remembered certain people who I supposedly knew from my childhood – friends and acquaintances from my pre-indoctrination life.

"Do you know a man named Johnny Walsh?"

"Yes, of course I do, I went to school with him -" My answer – made without thinking – shocked me. My words were automatic – I actually had no memory of this person. Hughes looked surprised also.

"You do actually remember Johnny Walsh then?" he repeated. I thought hard.

"Nope – I definitely do not remember Johnny Walsh – not as a person anyhow – maybe the name rings a bell"

"OK, what about Art Mercer?"

"The words sound familiar but that's all" Hughes scribbled something into his notebook. He took a deep breath before continuing.

"Ever heard of Mark Hopkins?"

I reacted violently – like some big red button had been pressed in my psyche – you know, the one which says 'Do Not Press'...

A typhoon of rage blasted through my brain – unleashing immensities of violence which had been secretly on simmer for longer than I could possibly remember. I sprang out of my chair and grabbed Captain Hughes by the throat. We both fell to the floor where I began banging his head violently on the carpet, my hands gripping tighter and tighter in an attempt to crush his windpipe.

A door opened. Two big hairy sergeants grabbed me roughly by the arms and threw me down into a chair.

"Don't fucking move a muscle pal!". I slumped. Saw what had happened – my senses finally catching up with the situation.

"Oh my God – I'm so sorry Captain – I literally didn't know I was attacking you". The captain was a pretty tough character and soon pulled himself together – rubbing his throat with one hand.

"You weren't attacking me Old Chap, you were trying to kill Mark Hopkins". I thought it brave of him to mention that name again, considering what had transpired last time. This time, there was no reaction.

"Mark Hopkins, Mark Hopkins" I mumbled – the name obviously was an important one to me somehow. Judging by how I had reacted I could only assume that Mark Hopkins was not my favourite person. "Again, the name yes, the man, no".

"It'll come back to you in time, Michael – and don't feel bad about what happened – I should have been more cautious".

"Well that's very magnanimous of you Captain – I don't know what came over me".

"I do" he replied. "All will be made clear to you very soon"

"That'd be nice" I quipped.

Chapter 6

I slept a lot during the next few days – partly because my brain was working overtime, partly due to some little grey pills I was given. My mind was swirling all over the place, my dreams chaotic, confused and sharp-edged.

Once the worst was over, I was 'allowed' to stay awake during the day, to read magazines – even watch some dull programmes on TV. The boredom was a good sign they said. I guess it made sense.

Towards the end of the week, Captain Hughes appeared back on the scene. He showed me photographs of people. I was supposed to guess who they were. When I failed to do so, Hughes told me anyway – I suppose they wanted to see if looking at the pictures would have any emotional or psychological effect on me before they put names to the faces.

"That's Art Mercer" Hughes handed me a photo of a man who looked nothing if not mediocre – he wore mechanics' overalls. The photo was taken from a high position, zooming down on the subject. The man was not aware that his picture was being taken. He was standing next to a piece of equipment – possibly some sort of marine engine.

"His face does seem kinda familiar, I suppose"

"Nothing more than that?"

"Nope"

"Try this one again – Johnny Walsh. He was your best friend at school and you've been best friends on and off ever since".

The image showed another man wearing overalls. Maybe I only knew mechanics in my former life. However, this time something clicked.

"I know this one – yes – Johnny Walsh – that's it – I definitely remember the face and I know his name is Johnny Walsh".

"Do you remember anything else about him?"

"It's a bit confusing – school things when we were kids – mucking about, that sort of thing – but – also – some sort of boat – and ..."

"Don't force it Michael – the memory will come back in it's own time. Its good that you remember things about him though – try this"

"Mark Hopkins?" I enquired

"Yes. Mark Hopkins" We both braced ourselves as I looked at the photo again. I had not recognised the man before I had been given the name – but now I knew the bastard – and I felt anger rise up again – not so much as before – I had no urge to attack Captain Hughes this time.

"Oh, yes – some of it is coming back to me – did he try to kill me?"

"Yes and no" replied Hughes, cryptically.

"Either he did or he didn't – which is it?" Hughes shrugged before replying.

"Well the truth is that Mark Hopkins never tried to kill you – or anybody else – but you will have strong memories which contradict that – it's because of the brainwashing – made you see Mark Hopkins when it was in fact somebody else"

"Oh, thanks, that's cleared things up nicely – NOT!" Hughes couldn't help smiling to himself.

When he saw my darkening visage he wisely decided to stop smiling.

"Sorry Michael – I know it sounds strange but they used what's called an 'overlay' method on you. Its a way of getting people to do what you want by programming them to see someone they know instead of the actual person they are with. They linked your mind to one of their agents – made you see him as Mark Hopkins – that agent was the man who tried to kill you and caused you so much trouble. The real Mark Hopkins knows nothing about any of this"

"Unbelievable" I muttered "I suppose the actual Art Mercer and Johnny Walsh were not involved either?"

"That is correct. The people who worked on you knew that you would be much more amenable to manipulation by people you knew and trusted, so it was just a case of inducing an overlay in your mind via the advanced IPCRESS process and bingo!."

"I became a puppet."

"You were made to believe that Mark Hopkins was behind it all and later they made you believe Johnny Walsh was the real villain".

"But it was actually agents of G10 pulling my strings? - sounds like something out of a movie"

"It may sound incredible but its true Michael"

"I believe it" I replied, before relapsing into a stunned silence.

"The fact is Michael" Hughes spoke with his serious voice now, "Most of the things you have experienced as happening to you over the past couple of years have been mental projections – placed into your memory by G10. They have been making you remember things which never happened. They also created deep psychological overlays so that the images you were programmed with showed you interacting with people you knew well – ensuring you accepted the events more deeply and with less resistance. Their methods have moved on incredibly since the 1960s when the first IPCRESS programs were developed by a man named Eric Ashley Grantby. They now have financial backing worth billions and some of the shadiest stakeholders on the planet. There are also links to dark, secretive departments and sub-departments within legitimate national governments. Its a major threat to world order"

"So why would they be interested in me then?" I asked – not really wanting to know the answer.

"Sorry to say it Michael but you were no more than one guinea pig among thousands – it was the fact that you were an ordinary man with few social contacts and no important social positions that appealed to them"

"You mean they practice on 'nobodies' like me because no-one is likely to notice or care if we go missing"

"That's about the size of it" replied Captain Hughes, glumly.

"Then why did you go to all the trouble of rescuing me – if I'm so worthless?"

"The mere fact that you had undergone extensive programming by them, made you a valuable asset to us – we are still learning about what they are up to and each person we rescue gives a clearer picture regarding how they work and what they do – you will be comprehensively debriefed once it has been established that your memories are sufficiently back online, so to speak, that your psyche has re-gained sufficient stability to cope with the long term interrogation we need to put you through in order to get as much information about your case as possible"

"So months or years of non-stop questions is to be my future is it?" I tried to be angry but managed only a sense of defeat and fatigue.

"There are upsides to the debriefing for you Mike – by going through everything in minute detail you will gain a much clearer picture of what has happened to you - further stabilising your sense of identity which has been badly damaged by the G10 processing"

"I'm not sure how much of it I can help you with – my memories are still very partial"

"That's to be expected – we still need to give you all the information we have – it should help fill in some gaps for you – which in turn will help you to fill in some gaps for us – its a two-way conversation – not an interrogation"

"When do we start?"

"In a few days – after you've had time to assimilate what you have remembered and learnt today – we must not overload your brain – its still coming to terms with events and slowly switching off the protective barriers it erected to preserve the integrity of your persona"

You mean my memories were shut down to stop me from going completely insane"

"Yes, that's one way of putting it. The human brain is an incredibly sophisticated piece of equipment with many built-in security and protection systems".

"Will I ever get back to my old self?" I asked – again not really wanting to know the answer.

"Everything that happens to a person in their life changes what they are and how they see the world – so you will not be the same person in that sense – but we believe that the underlying integrity of your subconscious and your personality is intact and will become re-established to a high degree – so yes, you will still be the old you – but maybe a bit older and wiser"

"That's something at least" I sounded bitter and deflated – which was how I felt. Hughes stood up.

"I think we've done enough for today – best get you some food and fresh air – and some much-needed sleep Old Chap"

"Sounds great" I mumbled.

Chapter 7

It took me a while to come to terms with the fact that most of the memories which began to resurface over the next few weeks were in fact false memories, implanted into my mind by some outrageous brainwashing system. It was a strange feeling, knowing that things I remembered doing – as clear as crystal – were in fact things I had not actually done. People I began to remember doing those things with me, had not in fact been present or even aware of those actions. Even the actions I remembered doing with the people who were not actually there, hadn't, in the most part, happened at all. And yet I remembered them.

Until now I had not realised just how much our sense of identity – or who we are – is so deeply and inextricably linked to our memories. In fact it could be said that as far as you are concerned – you *are* your memories and little else. To others, you are your behaviour and nothing else. I was starting to understand just how subtle and powerful the IPCRESS processing, which I had undergone at the hands of the mysterious and dangerous G10 organisation, had been.

Hughes told me that my fate – if I had not been rescued, would have been death and a quick burial. It was the habit of G10 to push their subjects as far as possible until their minds broke – and then dispose of them. I had been in the last phase of processing before I became worthless to them – my mind had shut down my memory – and rendered me useless.

During my 'treatment' I had been programmed to believe I was hunted by the police for murders of my friends. My friends knew nothing of this and were still living their old lives – wondering where their old buddy Mike had disappeared to, carrying on oblivious to all I had thought I was experiencing with them. Johnny Walsh had not been murdered by Me, Art Mercer or even Mark Hopkins – he was still fixing his classic Ford Anglia as usual. Art was still living in the same rambling property, selling marine supplies and fixing engines. Mark Hopkins was still involved in several shady small-time semi-legal activities – including 'importing' smoking materials from the continent. They all wondered why I had suddenly disappeared off the face of the earth but carried on without me.

I learned that there were no such people as Liam Harries, Inspector Glaze or General Willings. There was no Red Boat. No nuclear explosions. I had never been to Lithuania.

I had however been inside a vast 'processing centre' where extensive false memories had been implanted. Memories which I had now recovered and which still felt completely real even though I knew they were not. By breaking down my sense of identity – which had never been that strong in the first place – by inducing traumatic ideas into my psyche which caused tension, fear and a sense that I was losing what little grip on reality I had, they had controlled me. As my sense of who I was became weaker and my sense of fear grew, I became more susceptible to the new concepts they planted into my mind – people will clutch at any straw when they are on the brink of insanity – it is stability they crave more than anything else – it matters not what they believe as long as it is consistent. So they gave me some new, consistent beliefs, inserted these ideas into parts of the brain which control memory.

It was an important element of their brainwashing, reprogramming system, that the balance between confusion and fear on the one side and the introduction of new memories on the other, was adjusted within certain effective parameters. This was the reason they kept switching things around on me – like who they made me believe was behind G10 – it maintained a fog of confusion. The way they made me believe that Johnny Walsh had been killed – then he had faked his own killing. Liam Harries was a cop – then a cop killer – then a high-ranking officer in Army intelligence. Mark Hopkins was a goody, then a baddy - then dead, then alive again. It seemed incredible now that I had believed all of this, experienced it all as reality, when in fact it had been nothing more than a psychedelic picture show inside my abused and disoriented mind. Even little things like the sudden appearance of the G10 warehouse near to my home in Norfolk and the supposed killing of Tony Smith had been tests of my pliability – little tweaks and flourishes created by the evil geniuses behind my torment.

I had not even lived in Norfolk as it turned out – there was no Tony Smith. I was still officially resident in my crummy 2 bed semi in a housing estate in Winchester, though according to enquiries made by Hughes, this too was going to end soon as the mortgage company were in the process of repossessing the property because I had not been paying the mortgage. What savings I'd had, had finally run out and the Direct debits were no longer being paid by my bank. So no house and no savings either. I didn't care one jot about any of it. I was just glad to be getting better – coming to terms with the enormity of what had happened, relieved that I had been finally rescued by the military department who now, slowly, were restoring me to near normality.

I had been given very little information regarding exactly who these military people were – they looked like British soldiers and acted the part – I was willing to go along with it for now – after all I had to believe something in order to function as a person and the things they were telling me were a lot better than what I had been told whilst in the clutches of G10.

Chapter 8

I spent the next few months answering questions. The powers that be had decided my mental state was now sufficiently healed and strong enough to begin the official debriefing process.

I cooperated fully with this tedious procedure, which at times almost drove me crazy – the same questions over and over – with me giving the same answers. It was excruciating. There was an upside to all this however. With each repetition of the questions and answers, things became more solidified in my mind – creating a resilient foundation of identity for me to build on.

It was not all one way either – I discovered just how much of my previous three years had been falsified – for example I was shown photographs and film footage of Johnny Walsh going about his daily business - evidence which had date and time signatures attached to the media I was shown. Johnny going into a newsagents with a sign board declaring headlines which proved to be current news items, was just one way they backed up what they told me. There were many others. I came to fully accept that the lives of Johnny Walsh and Art Mercer were carrying on as they always had done. It was obvious that none of them were dead – or in anyway masterminding some sort of international crime syndicate or military intelligence operation.

I was shown photographs of my sister Kirsty and her two sons – all looking older now, still acting in normal ways in Southampton. I was informed that I would soon be able to speak to Kirsty, possibly even visit her.

A month later I telephoned her – the call had been carefully prepared in advance – Captain Hughes had primed her and answered her questions regarding my disappearance. Specifically what he had told her was unclear to me but she asked me no awkward questions – just sounded relieved I was alive and pleased to hear my voice. I felt a little uncomfortable at first but soon got the impression that my sister understood I had been the victim of others, that my disappearance had not been voluntary. Her enthusiasm cheered me immensely – reinforced my growing links to reality – made me feel I was returning to my true place in the world.

A few weeks later I was driven to Southampton and met with Kirsty – the boys were not present – she hugged me so strongly, she almost cracked a couple of ribs. The visit lasted two hours – Kirsty had baked some sausage rolls which I dutifully – and rather greedily - scoffed with abandon. We chatted about nothing in particular – I was more than happy to listen to her spout the type of inane local gossip which would previously have sent me running for the exit. To get a picture of a normal person's life – their prosaic and local actions and events made me feel real, strong and optimistic about my future – I had been released from a dark dungeon of confusion, fear, unpredictability, danger and shock. I was no longer the plaything of forces too strong to resist – or so I hoped.

My often asked question of "Why Me?" had also finally been answered – it was because I was a loner, a loser – the sort of person nobody would miss or care about for long. I wasn't special, I was just fodder for the G10 machine to play with and spit out. I was not the Prime Minister – had never been wanted for killing my friends – never been up to Whitehall to speak to generals – never been on a super-secret boat which was also an atomic bomb – never been to Latvia – never been on the Moon or fought aliens. I had not bought a cottage in Norfolk, not been abducted in the Channel by Stripey and Drowny, not had my boat rammed - or been to St.Malo or Norway.

These memories were completely false – fictions perpetrated on me, forced into my mind by sophisticated brainwashing techniques. Many others had suffered the same fate – suffered the same abuse. There were hundreds who had been murdered, thrown into seas or deep pits like unwanted rubbish – once their minds had cracked and they were no longer of use to the psychopaths behind G10.

Each time I went through the questions and answers I saw a little more clearly that everything I had experienced from the moment I got a phone call from Johnny Walsh, right up until I was finally rescued by Captain Hughes, had been false. I was now cleared of the belief that these things had actually happened – though I did still retain clear memories of what those false things were and had strong feelings, based upon those memories, of those events actually happening. I was not likely to forget these memories for a long time – I had to remind myself that the feelings were based on false memories and learn to ignore them. It was a strange and difficult way of living life – but it got easier with time and after a year in the army facility I was told I would soon be turned loose – set free to live as a fairly normal human being once again. With support and monitoring of course. To be honest I was glad of the support and monitoring. I was frightened of relapsing if left to my own devices too much.

It had been decided that I was to live in a nicely appointed flat in Southampton – not far from my sister's house. The apartment had security doors and video cameras outside. There was a slight concern that G10 would attempt to get hold of me, to re-establish control over me – to test their techniques against the deprogramming given to me by my new friends.

I was given emergency numbers to call if I felt my sanity slipping away. I would also be set up in a job – something regular and unchallenging, to help consolidate my new ordinary existence.

The apartment was owned by the government. It had been used to help re-establish other victims of G10 who had been saved. I was told never to discuss anything that had happened to me with other residents – or anyone else for that matter - including my sister. I had to live as my new self and not contact any of my old acquaintances. I was a little dubious about this as Art Mercer lived in Southampton and Johnny Walsh not far away. I was reassured that if I stuck to the dull routine and kept my head down, I would be fine. I was to stay there for a year. I would then be set up in another town – with more freedom.

My little boat – *Beach Boy* – was considered too much of a link to my brainwashing and was sold on my behalf. Once my trial period was over I would be supplied with a replacement boat and paid a substantial compensation package for the suffering I had gone through – after all it was a failure of British Intelligence to shut down G10 that had led to my abduction and abuse – it seemed only fair that I get enough resources to restart my life in at least as good a position as I had been living when the persecution began. I could choose where I wanted to live and the authorities would do the rest. I had a lot to look forward to.

My year in Southampton was as tedious as it had been planned to be. I worked in a local supermarket – shelf stacking and storeroom duties. I enjoyed it. It made me feel ordinary which was the thing I craved. I spent time with Kirsty and my nephews, mainly chatting about how the boys were doing at school and Kirsty's job. I also talked about my shop work and ventured no further. It was dull and wonderful. I was however, relieved when the year was up. Kirsty had been prepared for my departure, accepting it as a positive development in my rehabilitation – I think she was getting a bit fed up with having me pop round all the time – can't say I blame her. I was the most boring man ever to exist in the history of life on earth.

Chapter 9

As the time came for me to be 'set free' to make my own choices, I began thinking that maybe I didn't want to live in England any more – I had never really been a success here and there were too many bad memories linked to the British Isles.

I considered various locations around the world but none seemed to fit the bill. I didn't want to be tied down to a single location, had no reason for being at any particular place at any particular time. So I decided I would live on a boat – a seagoing home I could grow old gracefully in – maybe finding somewhere I belonged, a far away island in the pacific or unknown stretch of ocean.

I discussed the idea with Hughes, who seemed to be my ongoing 'case worker'. He had some concerns – mainly that I might be found by certain 'bad actors' who might still be interested in me. I pointed out that I would be harder to find if I was pottering about in the world's oceans than a sitting target in a flat in Southampton.

He acquiesced at this point and arrangements were made to help me find a boat which would suit my requirements. I could choose any boat I desired, with a purchase price considerably above what my little house would have been worth – this was partly to be viewed as compensation, though there was a promise that I would receive a considerable payment over and above this within a few months, as soon as an 'official assessment' had been completed. This money would appear in my bank account forthwith and I would be comfortable enough to pursue my sailing life for a considerable time period without the need to worry about how it was going to be financed.

This was more than I had expected. I began to feel excited about my future for the first time – possibly ever. I spent time visiting boatyards and reading sailing magazines – trawling the small ads in search of that perfect boat which would become my 'forever home'.

I had to undergo a final bit of debriefing – mainly they just wanted to check that I was sane enough, stable enough, to make a fair start to my new life. They told me they planned to release me completely from their control. I would not be monitored once I left their care – I was going to be a normal, ordinary person again. I was slightly anxious about this – which was to be expected after everything I had gone through – but looking forward to finally regaining my freedom.

Eventually I found the boat I had been searching for. It was for sale at a rather elevated price and although an old design, it was in excellent condition, having been kept moored for the past seven years and in dry dock for much of its life.

Built way back in the early 1980s – The Westsail 32 was a heavy-displacement sailboat designed for ultimate seaworthiness. She was massively constructed, fitted with a comfortable, roomy interior. These sailing craft had circumnavigated the globe many times – had won global sailing races and proved strong enough to survive the roughest oceans – even capsize on numerous occasions. They could be run single-handed and had enough storage to stay out at sea for extended periods.

I arranged via Hughes to visit the boat which was currently in Poole Harbour and I decided there and then that this was the craft I wanted to spend the foreseeable portion of my life in. After a short trial around the harbour and a thorough inspection of the back-up diesel engine, I arranged for payment and took possession of my new home. The name painted on the side was *'Black Moon'*

I had to wait a couple more weeks before I could take her out to sea proper – there were last minute 'assessments' and advice to contend with, but by the start of summer I was free to live as a human being again.

As the Land Rover driven by Hughes disappeared into the distance, I stood on the jetty beside my new boat and sighed in absolute relief that the extended nightmare I had undergone was finally over.

I climbed aboard and went below. The comfortable lounge area was peaceful and well appointed. The galley had been stocked up with provisions, the fridge filled with delicacies. I wasted no time in getting myself a celebratory meal and drink. The Captain Morgan Spiced rum had never tasted better and the ham sandwich was down my neck in seconds flat. Michael Garvie was back!

Chapter 10

I spent an hour sailing around the harbour – getting acquainted with the workings of my new boat, raising and lowering the sails, which were designed to allow single-handed operation. The big Perkins/Volvo diesel engine had enough power for my needs. I checked the fuel tanks, water tanks and cupboards before setting off. The storage space below decks was vast. I had everything I could possibly require on my inaugural journey.

I gently throttled the engine as I slowly negotiated my way around Brownsea Island, through the narrow channel between Shell Bay Beach and Sandbanks, before moving into the English Channel.

After so long away from my previous craft - *Beach Boy* – I found it exhilarating and liberating to be back out in deep water once more. I raised my sails – which were configured in a cutter style - with a single mast, mainsail, forestay and jib – and enjoyed the light breeze pulling the boat smoothly through the water.

The heavy keel and overall structure of this boat were legendary – they added enormous strength and safety which were rare in a boat this small, although top speed was reduced – this model of boat had often been referred to by the nickname 'WestSnail' in certain yachting circles.

I was in no hurry to be anywhere, so this suited me fine. I drifted gently towards the centre of the Channel, enjoying a light snack and a bottle of cold beer from my overstuffed fridge. Sitting on deck, watching seagulls, the occasional craft in the distance and the lapping of the water from the spreading wake made by *Black Moon* as she slipped slowly through the sea, made me sleepy. I dozed off intermittently, spent a couple of hours thinking of nothing at all.

I slept well that night, anchored away from the main shipping lanes, everything battened down. The gentle rocking of calm seas worked it's slumberous spell upon me and I awoke late next morning, refreshed and happy.

I had long been considering my first port of call, once I had finally been set free. One idea, despite my consistent and intense efforts to push it away, would not leave me. It began to form the basis of a compulsion. I had to see for myself the things I had now become convinced were the final truth of my reality. I needed to see things with my own eyes as the final arbiter of what was real.

To this end, I set a course for Dover. I needed to visit the White Cliffs pub – if indeed such a place actually existed. I would not be able to rest until I had separated the facts from the fiction. I set my sails accordingly, caught a stiffening breeze as I headed to my appointed destination.

I felt tense at the thought of what might happen, anxious that I was doing the one thing most likely to start my mind shutting down again but it was absolutely imperative for my future sanity and confidence that I do this.

The morning was warm, breezy and bright. The trip itself took only a couple of hours and by around noon I was moored at the outer edge of Dover Harbour. As I approached land I saw in the distance a white building situated on the cliff top over to my left. It looked like the pub. It unnerved me a little to see that the place actually existed – part of me had been hoping that the White Cliffs pub was simply an imaginary location which had been brainwashed into my psyche, and would not actually exist.

I took a taxi from the harbour up the hill upon which the pub was perched. As we pulled into the car park, I saw the sign which declared the place to be 'The White Cliffs' public house. My hand shook as I paid the taxi driver – he gave me a rueful smile - no doubt thought I was suffering from the shakes and desperate for a drink. He was partly right – I definitely did need a drink. I took a deep breath, opened the main door of the pub. 'Here Goes' I thought - 'Shit or Bust'.

The interior of the pub looked exactly as I 'remembered' it. This in itself was a shock to me. I had expected it to look different – just some sort of 'made up' film set which had been used to inject false memories into my mind – but no, it was like I had never left.

Even more shocking was the face of the man standing behind the bar – looking directly at me. Dermot Leach.

I almost staggered, had to grab hold of a table to steady myself. Dermot's face showed dislike at this – he probably thought I was half pissed.

"Can I help you sir?" his voice contained a slight edge of disapproval. I walked calmly – and steadily - to the bar, smiled at Dermot – who managed to smile back.

"A pint of your best bitter, please" I almost added the phrase 'my good man' but managed to refrain from such extreme bonhomie – it would have convinced him I was well trolleyed and I didn't want to create a bad impression.

As he began to pour my pint, Dermot seemed to relax a little. "Not seen you in here before sir, are you a visitor to Dover?"

"Just passing through – I'm a sailor upon the seven seas, new in town and not stopping long"

"We do get a lot of nautical travellers in here from time to time, Sir" he replied. He showed absolutely no sign of recognising me and I was convinced that he was not acting. He had never set eyes on me before. It was weird to recognise him and his pub while at the same time knowing I had never in reality – whatever that was – been here before. I remembered it but what I was remembering was false – Dermot's face no doubt one of the sinister 'overlays' used by G10 to make me feel I knew him. I would never get used to remembering things which had never happened. It wasn't nice.

I paid, took my pint over to a little table by the window. I sat looking out into the car park – another clear memory which existed only in my mind. I half expected Mark Hopkins to turn up in his Mercedes or his blue smuggling van. I was very glad that he didn't. Just being here in this setting was enough for me to cope with for now.

I lit up a cigarette – I was back on them again. I inhaled deeply, felt a strengthening of my resolve. I had made my first foray into reality – into truth. Even after all the reassurances and proof I had been given by Captain Hughes over the past months, I still needed to verify things for myself. Only then would I be able to relax and integrate myself into life as it really was. Only then would I feel completely cured.

Coming here, to the White Cliffs was just the beginning of a long corroborative process I had to undergo – under my own steam – no input, advice, guidance or support would be helpful. I wanted to be freed of all outside influence, both good and bad. Only by seeing things with my own eyes – finding out how things actually stood in the real world, could I regain my full sanity, reclaim my true identity. Only then would I feel confident in making decisions about my future.

I sipped the pint, my mind slightly dazed, my eyes only semi-focused on my surroundings, before ordering a refill and a steak & kidney pie. In my memory, the food served here had been excellent – I wanted to see if it really was.

Ten minutes later my food arrived, piping hot. The pastry was soggy – no doubt it had been warmed in a microwave. The meat – what there was of it – was fatty and unpleasant. I laughed out loud, strangely pleased with my awful dinner.

I ate as much of it as was edible and left the carcase on the plate. One more cigarette, a necked pint and a slash and I was back outside and nosing around the car park.

Nothing strange, unusual or particularly memorable here, although the rear doors were the same as I remembered them, which I found a little disappointing for some reason. Maybe I wanted everything to be different from what I had been programmed to remember. This was an unreasonable hope, considering the brainwashing had been based upon actual people and places.

I decided to walk back down to the harbour – it was only a couple of miles and the weather was nice – warm and bright, without being too sunny. Good walking weather.

It took me almost an hour to get back to my boat after a couple of detours down side streets and through a small shopping centre, made just for the sense of freedom it gave me to be able to go wherever I liked, for no particular reason.

Once onboard, I made myself a quick ham sandwich and washed it down my gullet with a glass of milk. Then I was ready for my next port of call – and my next reality check.

I spent the night in the harbour, reading nautical charts, drinking a lot of Captain Morgan's Spiced Rum. I slept well.

It was a bit drizzly next morning when I set off. The wind had picked up a little too, which helped fill my sails. I thoroughly enjoyed the short sailing, getting used to the rigging of the *Black Moon*, which was new to me. The set up made it easy to adjust sail positions single-handedly and I began to see why the Westsail 32 had made a name for itself as a solo circumnavigator of the globe.

I arrived at Southampton Docks just before noon, tied my boat up to the jetty. I knew this town well and jumped on a bus which would take me to within yards of Art Mercer's place.

The building was lit up, fully operational – a marked contrast to the last time I had seen it in my false memory – when it had been boarded up and silent – part of the proof that Art had been killed.

I was surprised, not shocked – I had become somewhat used to unexpected events, had developed a level of immunity to emotional overreaction. I peered into the main window of the garage area, saw two men working on a car, their backs to me. They both wore dark blue overalls.

Even from behind, I recognised Art Mercer – his unkempt grey hair was one of his trademark features. Art Mercer was alive, doing what he had always done – in the place where he had always done it. It came as a massive relief to me. I felt years of tension, fear and worry dropping away as I now had proof that I had indeed been fed a false memory. Captain Hughes had shown what proof he could, but actually seeing Art Mercer back to life and normality, gave me a whole new level of hope for the future.

This sense of elation lasted all of ten seconds, until the second man turned partially in my direction. I almost cried out. I somehow managed to control myself. Here was shock in the extreme. Standing five yards away, the other side of the window, was a perfect clone of myself. I ran. I kept running. Then a pub. Then oblivion.

Chapter 11

I awoke sometime around noon the next morning – I had managed to find my way back to the *Black Moon*. My head hurt like hell. I had grazed my left arm. My throat was extremely sore from all the cigarettes I had smoked. Then the memory of what I had seen came crawling back into my frazzled brain and I cried out in horror. They had made a clone of me – he was living my life, interacting with all my friends, fully accepted by them. Nobody was wondering what had happened to poor old Mike Garvie – as far as they were concerned Mike was still going about his business as before – no change to his routine, personality or behaviour!

It was incredible – even after all the things I had undergone and learned concerning the manipulations of reality – the brainwashing, the IPCRESS processing centres, the fake memories – all of it – this was a completely unexpected turn of events which opened a whole new – and very nasty – can of worms. My mind was under intense pressure – my sense of who I was, had been completely shattered again – and I was outraged that they would create a doppelgänger of me and let it take over my life.

How was this even possible? Did nobody notice any little changes in 'Michael Garvie's' behaviour, see no gaps in his knowledge of the minutiae of past interactions – there was no way that anyone could have known all the little childhood events I had shared with my friends – there must have been errors, unusual responses, from the clone which would have caused people to notice the change – even my sister must be interacting with this copy of me – surely Kirsty would know the difference?

And then it hit me – the reason nobody had noticed any subtle changes in the words or actions of the Michael Garvie copy was because *He* was not the copy – I was! I was the clone.

I had been taken to see my sister, just before my release, to see if she would accept me as her brother. They told her I must not be questioned about my experiences as it could upset my mental equilibrium – she would have written off any little lapses in memory or strange behaviours as symptoms of my trauma.

My problem with this line of thought was explaining how she had been told that I had undergone deep psychological problems, while at the same time she had been interacting with the real Michael Garvie. He would, at some point, visit her and would deny all knowledge of what he had, according to her, undergone. It was possible that they had impressed upon her to never mention or refer to these alleged problems again – telling her that it was imperative that she act like it had never happened in order to avoid causing me to relapse. That could work. I knew Michael didn't visit her often – No, I didn't – I only knew what I had been programmed to know – maybe the 'real' Michael Garvie visited his sister all the time. It was too confusing to figure out, so I sank a whole bottle of

Captain Morgan's Spiced, went into a self-inflicted temporary coma.

For the next two days I kept myself sedated, stewed, insensible. I could not cope with the things I knew so I blotted them out as best I could. This was only partially successful for my alcohol-induced dreams tore at my sanity just as powerfully as my waking moments.

After two days I ran out of booze. I gradually sobered up. My body had not been fed properly for nearly 72 hours and I was in need of a shower. My chin had sprouted stubble, my hair was a matted nest and I smelled like the inside of a ferret's cage.

I spent the day rectifying these matters and by early evening I was in some semblance of civilised order – at least on the outside. Inside I was a maelstrom of raging, chaotic emotions, my head filled with confusion, insecurity and depression. I had to find out who I was – and find out fast, before my mind caved in and my will to live ceased altogether.

I decided to get back out to sea – it would give me the space and time I required to come to terms with these latest revelations, make some sort of plan as to how I might respond – if at all – to what I had discovered.

Early next morning – before it was properly light, I set out, entering the English Channel once more – again wracked with confusion and mystery concerning reality and my place in it.

I was beginning to think that the Dover area and certain reaches of the Channel were cursed – at least as far as I was concerned – the bad memories – whether real or fake – associated with this stretch of water and its nearby land masses, far outweighed any good ones I could bring to mind. It was not a location I felt to be conducive to my health to remain in if I had any choice, and I now had that choice. I did not have to react to everything by taking dramatic actions or descending into mental chaos. I had the option of ignoring it all by going my own way – even if I did not know what my way was because I did not know who I was.

Or did I? I may not know my legal name, or have a job, a place in society, or any friends. I may not be able to trust others, believe what I saw with my own eyes, or what anyone told me, but I was alive, I was free. I had a boat which could take me anywhere in the world. I had plenty of money. I could live quite happily for many years without the need to play the games of whoever it was that had been playing games with me. I had the option to opt out. They had ruined my life and stolen my identity – but my life had been dull and pointless and my identity that of a nobody, a loser. So maybe they had done me a favour in the long run.

I could decide who I was, what I stood for and where I went in order to stand for it. I was as free as a bird – a newborn baby – with all the resources I required for as long as I required them. In many ways I was in an ideal position.

If I chose to start my life – to be reborn – starting from the here and now, from the position I was currently in – I could be anything, go anywhere. A whole new lease of life.

I cut my jib accordingly, sailed off into the proverbial sunset.

Chapter 12

The *Black Moon* was performing well. Her strong keel progressed smoothly through the sea. Slow, steady advancement was made – my craft cutting through the water like a silky dolphin.

I had gotten used to the necessary manipulations for furling and unfurling my sails and was now in full command of my vessel. The diesel engine had been put through its paces and proved itself strong and reliable. The equipment and supplies which filled the wide keel contained everything which may be required under any normal circumstance which might occur. We were off and running and it felt good.

Only once did the weather turn rough – we were passing Lundy island. I lowered the sails, slowed until the minor storm passed. *Black Moon* took it in her stride, as did I.

The next two weeks were idyllic – the weather was bright, with enough breeze to use the sails. We turned North up the Irish Sea. After a couple of very restful weeks sailing I decided to make a stop – just for a change of scenery.

I moored my vessel at Port St. Mary, near the southern point of the Isle of Man and walked the mile or so to the Shore Hotel at Gansey, booking in for one night. The place was well appointed, the food lived up to its reputation. I slept well and rose refreshed. I watched birds flapping about on the seashore, walked on the sand for a bit, and stopped for a pint at a little inn I discovered in a cove along the way.

By late afternoon I was back aboard my boat, pulling out into the Irish Sea. A pleasant interlude, which brought to my mind a train of thought which had been slowly growing and which I had been doing my best to ignore. It was all well and good floating about the world's oceans, enjoying myself – and I definitely deserved some pampering time after my trials and tribulations – but I couldn't help feeling that however pleasurable it might be – it was also rather aimless. I knew I would tire of it fairly quickly. I needed a purpose. My brain required some form of goal. I could think of no such aim. I became restless, dissatisfied. In fact I became angry. I began to feel cheated – I had achieved my desire for wealth and freedom – and it bored me.

I either had to find a challenge which meant something to me or go back to my old life – with all its inherent mystery and danger.

Maybe some rougher seas would calm my ennui. I sailed north-east through the Mull of Kintyre, into the sea area of Malin and on to Rockall. Here the North Atlantic became a little less friendly and I encountered a South-Westerly gale force 8 in which the sea became rough, possibly very rough, with occasional rain and fog patches - at least that was how it was described on the Shipping Forecast which the Met office issued during my time there.

The *Black Moon* took this in her stride – she creaked a bit, some of the fittings on deck tapped and rattled like they meant it – but my vessel shrugged it off – all in a day's work for her. I felt invigorated by the experience – though I did at one point fall on the deck after being hit by what is often termed a 'freak' wave – but which is quite normal under such conditions. A good-sized bump on the head and a sprained wrist were the price I paid for my clumsiness.

As day turned into night, the weather improved and I raised my sails again, turning North into Bailey, then East – cutting across the corner of Hebrides, into Faeroes. I was now due north of Scotland and the sea temperature was well down. It was very blustery. The experience of harsh – though not dangerous, weather at night on a sailing boat was one of the most magnificent events of my life. Although I had owned a few boats, pootled around in the Channel many times – I had never been anywhere serious as a solo yachtsman – if you discounted my fake memories of doing just that – which I did. I felt elated each time a large, freezing wave smashed itself to a hissing oblivion on the deck of my boat, almost laughing out loud as the icy spume and stiletto gusts cut through my clothing and washed me down, like a vicious Brillo Pad with a personal agenda. It was glorious.

By morning I was exhausted but elated. The power of nature, the smooth working of my superb boat, cutting through the water like a coal-black shark; the activity of staying on course, steering and adjusting as required, the top notch equipment, fixtures and fittings of the craft – created within me an urge - the goal I had been looking for. I knew that the boat I owned was a design made for solo round the world racing and travel – so I chose to follow in the wake of so many heroic people who had circumnavigated in this exact model of yacht. I would embark on a round the world trip and directly experience all of the world's oceans. The prospect terrified me – and excited me in equal measure.

I knew very little regarding how to undertake such an epic journey – nor did I want to know. I would simply set off and take each day as it came. I had nobody to consider but myself – if I capsized in a storm and drowned, it would be a perfectly acceptable way to go for a sailor – and I would join hundreds – if not thousands of other salty dogs in Davy Jones' Locker.

I passed through Fair Isle, into Forties with no major issues – apart from tiredness which increased as the seas became a little calmer. As I approached the Dogger Bank I trimmed my sails, snoozed at the wheel. I saw a few oil tankers moving between the North Sea oil fields, but nothing came close by. I was in no hurry.

It was getting dark as I approached the Humber Estuary, traversed Spurn Bight and moored at Grimsby.

I spent two days in the town, catching up on sleep, restocking my fridge and supply cupboards, topping up fuel and water tanks on my boat. I thoroughly checked my sails and rigging – which were unaffected by my recent stormy passage around Scotland. I bought myself some cold weather clothing, including some very expensive Neptune boots. I searched for – but could not find a yellow sou' wester.

I had some decent charts which covered most of Northern Europe and some good electronic navigation equipment installed – I should be fine as far as knowing where I was. The radio I had aboard was high quality – I hoped not to use it often but it would come in useful if I experienced any emergency situations. I felt ready to go. It would be the high point of my life. The only high point. I couldn't wait to get away from UK waters, sail towards whatever punishment or reward those famous 'Seven Seas' had planned for me.

At 6 o'Clock the next morning, the *Black Moon* moved out of Grimsby, back into the North Sea. I would not be back for a long time. I couldn't see any reason why I should come back at all.

I headed south, slowly sailing down the North Sea – back through the English Channel and finally three days later, rounding Ushant and passing into the North Atlantic Ocean.

Now I was in truly open water. I began to experience a lightening of the spirit, a clearing of the head. The weight gradually lifted from my shoulders.

I began to grow a beard. I began to smile often. I spent time watching the sea life which swarmed around me. I waved in a friendly manner to other vessels, especially the many European trawlers I encountered.

I had decided to head down past the Iberian peninsula – cutting between Portugal and the Azores, southwards towards the massive continent of Africa. Here I would find a quiet harbour and spend some time – maybe a week or two – on land – replenishing my food stores, water supplies and diesel fuel.

I spent four weeks peacefully travelling the 1500 miles – nothing of an adverse nature occurred – just one fairly bad storm which got a bit hairy for a few hours before fading away to be replaced by relatively calm oceans and increasingly hot sun as I approached the equatorial regions. I and my boat, coped admirably. I knew there would be other, more deadly seas and weather systems awaiting further south.

I docked in the tourist-infested Moroccan city of Casablanca and booked into a smart, modern hotel on the seafront. It was hot, noisy and I enjoyed my time there immensely. The Moroccan people are mostly very welcoming and delight in playing mischievous tricks on the uptight western tourists. I learned a few words of Arabic, ate some exotic foods, prepared in the hotel kitchens and served in the elaborate colonial dining room – my favourite being the Lamb Tagine – a stew literally named after the special pointy-lidded terracotta dish it was served in. I ate one almost every day whilst luxuriating in the hotel. I also spent time in the large swimming pool and took a few short trips around the local attractions with other people who were staying at the same hotel.

It was during my stay in these exquisite surroundings that I happened to glance at one of the English newspapers which, among similar offerings from around the world, was available daily in the hotel reception area. I read a headline stating that the British Prime Minister had been involved in a serious car accident and was being looked after in a private hospital in the countryside. Mr Shelton was expected to recover fully but unfortunately would require plastic surgery to repair some extensive facial injuries.

Reading the name Shelton unsteadied my nerves – I was horribly reminded of a time when I was told I was Mr Shelton, the Prime Minister. It was part of a game which somebody once played with me. I forced the memory away – it came back

– so I forced it away again. It was time to get back on my boat again. I hoped for extreme weather and high levels of danger – it was the only thing which made me feel alive these days – the only thing which kept the horrors completely at bay.

Chapter 13

I continued South for many days, the temperature and the seas began to rise as I progressed down the west coast of Africa. As I approached the Tropic of Cancer I observed a large shoal of sardines – an immense silvery display like nothing I had ever seen – a massive, flashing silver light-show, spreading a mile in every direction. I sipped Captain Morgan Spiced and snoozed as the *Black Moon* took care of business, slicing through the water as if she too were some big marine creature.

I had friendly, if sometimes mischievous, seas around me all the way to the Dakar peninsula in Senegal, where I made a stop at a well equipped harbour in Les Almadies, not far from the impressive King Fahd Palace Hotel. I decided to stay on my boat, not to splash out on hotel accommodation, although the facilities were top notch. I made use of their equipment though – the gym and pool area were quiet. I spent a couple of hours making use of them, along with the showers and restaurant. It was much hotter here, where the sea breezes didn't reach. I limited my movement, sitting on the sandy beach of Pointe des Almadies under an umbrella until the heat dissipated a little towards evening. I strolled along the sandy path which led to the furthest point west on the African mainland – a much hotter version of Land's End – and just as busy. I slept aboard, peacefully that night, took a taxi next morning to the Hypermarket at Yoff Airport, where I bought some more rum, ham and other fridge-based items.

I was back on my boat by mid-afternoon and headed back out to sea. I was approaching the Equator, and it was likely to get a lot warmer. I had not done enough research before I left Blighty to know what the seas would be like as I continued south – I was expecting it to get a little challenging. I looked forward to living on the edge. It was my new favourite thing.

Once I had settled my boat on auto pilot for the night, I switched on my powerful radio, tuned in to the BBC World Service in order to catch the latest shipping forecast. I was a little early for the programme, listened to the news reports which preceded it. Mostly boring political nonsense as usual. However there was mention of a massive terrorist attack on a British military base in the Hereford area which had taken place a few days previously. Some sort of missile had been aimed at the base and it had become inoperable – with extensive casualties.

Subsequently, there had been huge political fallout and the temporary leader of the government – filling in until Mr Shelton could return to parliament – had sacked the head of the Defence Ministry and replaced him with a General Willings.

I wondered if Captain Hughes was OK. I sipped some rum, listened to the Met office announcements regarding weather conditions off the West coast of Africa. Strong gales, heavy seas, possible hurricane conditions south of the Tropic of Capricorn. I would be approaching that area in a few days time and hoped the storms were still raging when I got there. I couldn't wait to feel alive again.

The ocean was smoother than expected as I reached – and passed – the Equator. The temperature out here, far away from the deserts and jungles of the continent – was considerably lower due to a fairly strong breeze. *Black Moon* zipped along, taking every little squall and minor gale with a pinch of salt. I was increasingly impressed with my vessel. She remained calm, while all around others would be losing their heads...

The skies got considerably darker as I neared the southern tropic. The waves turned nasty, with the help of unpredictable blasts of wind which seemed to come from every direction at once – twisting my boat in a yawing motion, almost causing me to fall overboard at one point. After that I put my bottle down and steered with both hands.

As the seas rose considerably, the winds became extreme, I began to feel alive. I began to feel free. My whole being – body and mind – were engaged in the most primal action of all – fighting to survive. There was no room for psychological inquiry, speculation, petty concerns – it was a case of living or dying – that was it. No complication involved. It was only here – at the very edge of existence, that I felt released from all my troubles.

The boat began to roll from side to side, pitch forward and back, yaw in a disconcerting corkscrew motion, as a major storm hit with little warning and no mercy. I held onto the rudder in a futile attempt to keep *Black Moon* on some kind of course – I was under engine power – it was far too dangerous to use my sails – they would have been ripped apart in minutes. I didn't take long to realise that the boat was in imminent danger of capsizing at any minute. I tied the rudder off. I was getting hit by some very strong waves, the likelihood of my being washed off the boat was increasing – so I went below, wedged myself between a pallet load of supplies and an inner bulwark which separated the cargo from the engine compartment. I would have preferred to remain up top but it was just too dangerous outside.

I had a bottle of Captain Morgan's Spiced rum in my hand and a growing sort of death-wish in my thoughts. I drank the hot burning liquid like it would be the last thing I would ever do and laughed at fate. The die was cast – it was shit or bust. I gave myself odds of 50/50. Would I pass through this immense storm alive or dead.? I put my money on dead.

Chapter 14

I lost. It was dark when I opened my eyes. It was also wet. I was lying in a pool of water, half way along the keel from where I had been ensconced when the storm got too rough to stay outside. The large pallet of provisions had been shifted, most of the contents had broken loose from the packing – there were tins of beans, toilet rolls and cartons of cigarettes floating on top of the flood – about four inches deep by my estimation. More water was trickling in through a hole in the hatchway which led to the upper deck – the storm had smashed and buckled it a little – but it still held.

I stood – the movement of the boat was considerably less than when I was last conscious of it. The gales had abated – the seas calmed to a heavy swell and the yawing had all but disappeared – though the boat was still pitching and rolling dramatically.

I stood, gripped the side of the keel until I could get my balance. It was not so much the dipping and bucking of the boat, as the amount of alcohol I had imbibed, which made standing difficult. I was still completely pissed.

I managed to stagger along until I reached the damaged hatch plate. I pushed it open and was rewarded with a shower of water which knocked me to the floor. I lay there in a waterfall for a couple of minutes, like an upturned crab, until the amount of water coming in began to subside – no doubt a lot had accumulated on the deck during the storm.

I clambered up the stairway onto the deck, sat with my back to a mast, observing the situation through drunken eyes. The main mast, which had been lowered and locked down onto the deck, was a little twisted out of position. This was due to its fittings being slightly bent. The mast itself looked fine. There was a lot of rope draped across everything – the supply store door had busted open – the deck looked like it had been invaded by giant snakes. I may have lost some rope overboard but it looked like most of it was still here. There was some other minor damage to fixtures and fittings, the jib had been torn at one corner, which was repairable.

As I sat there glassy-eyed, the weather improved as the light returned. I also improved – sobering up enough to think straight again – although I mainly thought about how much my head was beginning to hurt from all the booze I had sunk. At least the boat had not sunk, which was a relief, now that I was saner – and tired. I snoozed for a few minutes – sitting in a pool of water on the abused upper deck of my amazing boat. The *Black Moon* had survived almost fully intact, one of the most severe storms to hit this region for many years.

I went to my berth, which was dry – slept for three hours. I awoke feeling at least half human, and ravenously hungry. I went to the fridge – which had been locked and therefore had not spilled it's contents. I unlocked it, opened the door – it was a bit jumbled inside. A carton of milk had burst. It didn't take me long to put together a ham sandwich

71

and wolf it down, followed by a pint of milk from an unopened carton. Breakfast completed, I tidied the fridge and relocked it.

My thoughts were blurry, mainly due to the alcohol but also from the severe impact of the storm – and even more-so from the realisation that I was beginning to desire a violent death.

The initial elation I had felt when in a dangerous situation whilst in the storm north of Scotland, had grown and mutated into a desperate urge to keep my rage at bay. It had got to such a peak that the only way these overwhelming emotions could be dealt with was to put myself in a situation where I might be killed in a violent manner by extreme weather.

I had survived this latest tropical storm by the skin of my teeth. I was heading south towards Cape Horn – which would be even more dangerous – it was almost impossible for a boat as small as *Black Moon* to successfully round Cape Horn – many sailors had died trying to prove this statistic wrong – I was to be the next. Unless I chose another destiny.

I was running away, like I always did when things got tough. This time I had gone so far as to put my very existence in peril. It was the knowledge that I didn't know who I was – that I was a clone of another man, which tore at my very soul – tormented my mind, stirred up a maelstrom of negative emotion within me. I was literally nobody – just a husk – an experiment gone wrong – a copy of another man. If I chose to believe it. If I was willing to accept it. By running away, I had done exactly that. I had let them win.

I either had to let myself be killed – put my life on the line time and again until some weather formation got the better of me – or I had to reverse my decision, choose to confront everything that had happened and let fate choose if I lived or died as a result. I had to rip apart the wall of lies which had been constructed around me – I was unwilling to accept that I was not Michael Garvie. Regardless of all the evidence they had constructed to make me disbelieve it – I knew I was Michael Garvie. I had always been Michael Garvie. I would be Michael Garvie until the day I died – and for eternity thereafter.

Chapter 15

It took me a month to fight my way back through deadly seas and brutal winds. *Black Moon* creaked, shook and almost snapped under such appalling conditions but she came through with little more than superficial damage.

As I made my final approach into Dover harbour and moored my brave little boat, I knew I was a very different man to the one who had left, just a few months ago. My days of running away from danger and chaos were over. I would now be running towards it and I would be bringing chaos to anyone who got in my way. I needed a strong word with certain people. There were places I had to visit – things I needed to find out, to verify, check and challenge – I was not going to take any shit from anyone any longer. If I had previously been willing to die for no purpose in a sea storm, I would now be willing to die in order to re-assert and re-establish my identity as Michael Garvie. I couldn't care less what anyone else believed or said. I was choosing my own path through life now and I was willing to upset or even hurt anyone who stood in my way.

I paid the harbourmaster in advance for six months mooring – I may not be back here for some time and I wanted to ensure the *Black Moon* was safe where she was. I also arranged for a local boat guy to fix the minor damage my craft had sustained.

I was waiting outside the White Cliffs public house before it opened. As soon as the doors were unlocked I went in.

"You're keen mister – what'll it be?" Dermot Leach looked and sounded the same as when I had last seen him.

"A pint of lager and a bit of information"

"Well I can definitely help you with the pint – as for the information – I'll do what I can". He passed the glass across the bar to me. I paid him and took a long pull on the cold fluid.

"You may think I'm mad – who knows, maybe I am – but I want to ask you a strange question"

"Fire away pal" replied Dermot – no sense of suspicion or caution showed on his face. He looked a bit bemused at my behaviour but there was no sign of concern.

"Have you ever seen me before?" He studied my face for a few seconds before replying.

"Yes, I do believe you have been in here before – a couple of months or so maybe"

"And do you know who I am? What my name is?"

"Don't know your name – but pretty sure I've seen you in here"

"OK, thanks" I smiled to show my gratitude. "The reason I ask is that I have recently had an accident, been having a bit of memory loss – so I'm trying to get my bearings on a few things".

"Oh, I see"

"I've got one more question if you don't mind and then I'll leave you in peace"

"Fire away"

"Do you know a man named Mark Hopkins?"

"I doesn't ring any bells mate – I know a Paul Hopkins – tall blond guy – works in the fish market"

"No the one I'm thinking of is a huge ginger bugger"

"Can't help you there then mate, sorry"

"That's alright, it was a long shot". I went into a corner and sat at a small table, sipping my drink. After half an hour or so I left.

I was feeling unsure how to proceed – my plan had been to visit everyone who had been part of my imagined life and confront them. It now seemed an unproductive use of my time. There was however one person who I definitely did want to speak to – the guy who looked like me and who was last seen at Art Mercer's place.

I took a train to Southampton and was outside Art's garage just as it got dark. There was a light on in the main workshop and the office above. I marched straight in.

The place was full of doctors, nurses and beds – not a car or a mechanic in sight. I felt faint. A doctor in a white coat led me to a bed in a side room.

"Mr. Garvie, how nice to see you up and about" she said. I let her tuck me into the bed. She took my pulse. I fell asleep.

I awoke. I was in the bed. Nurse Susan was standing beside me, holding my hand – calling my name. I felt traumatised and confused.

"It's OK Michael – you're safe and well. How do you feel?"

"Weird. Where am I? Who are you? What's going on?" Nurse Susan chuckled.

"One question at a time Michael – I'm a nurse at the Dover General Hospital – my name is Susan and I have been looking after you for a long time".

I looked blank. "Why? Why am I in hospital?"

"I will go and fetch Doctor Preston – she has been in charge of your recovery"

Before I could argue – I didn't want to be left alone – the nurse went out of the room. She returned with a tall blonde woman in a white coat.

"Good Morning Michael" the woman said. "I am Doctor Preston – Stephanie – It's really great to see you awake and looking so well. I'm sure you must have a lot of questions and I will answer them all – but I'd just like to check a few things first – just to make sure you get well as quickly as possible".

"OK" I replied – I had no energy to argue – felt tired but also more normal than I had done for a while. The doctor took my pulse, felt my forehead, prodded, poked and studied the readout of some big machine to which I seemed to be attached. It scared me a bit, seeing this machine.

Doctor Preston – Stephanie – sat on a chair placed next to my bed and took my hand. "Michael, you have been here for a while – you have been in a trauma induced coma".

I just looked blank – the words didn't really make much sense to me.

"Just over a year ago, you were caught up in an incident in which you were injured. You went into a coma and have been unconscious in this hospital since then."

"How did I get here? Is my boat OK?" Why I asked these questions I didn't know – there was a lot of activity in my brain and it was swirling about.

"I've no idea about your boat Michael" Stephanie replied "but I can tell you that you were transferred here by ambulance directly after the incident which injured you". She looked at me intently assessing how much of the information she was giving me was sinking in. I nodded my head to let her know I was beginning to understand.

"What incident do you mean? I don't remember any incident".

"You will probably regain some memory about it in a while, but it is likely that you went into a coma before you had time to register what had happened, so you may never completely remember – this is quite normal in cases such as yours". I felt a bit annoyed at being referred to as a 'case' but said nothing. "You were at the docks in Dover – a bomb went off and you were caught in the pressure wave"

"I *have* been under pressure lately Doc – that's for definite" I managed a feeble smile to accompany my remark. Stephanie smiled – she seemed to take my witty comment as a good sign. I felt the confusion lessen slightly – though there was still plenty of it to go round. I was being told that I had been in an explosion, that I had been rushed to hospital in a coma – over a year ago. It was strange to be told this – but maybe not as strange as the things I had experienced while I was in the coma. I felt a sense of relief.

"You mean to tell me that I have been imagining all those terrible things, dreaming them all up?"

"I don't know anything about the experiences you have undergone whilst comatose – there is no way anyone but you would know that. I will arrange for Doctor Harries to talk you through your experiences – it will help you separate fact from fiction – but first we need to let you rest and get your strength up. Nurse Susan will get you something to eat later on – and I'll see if we can get you off this monitoring system soon and into a recovery bed."

I screamed. I screamed and kept on screaming. The doctor followed the direction of my eyes and saw that what had alarmed me to such a degree was the sign on the door – it said G10...

Chapter 16

The next time I awoke – after the sedative I had been given had done it's job – I saw that the number on the door was L9. I had been moved out of room G10 due to my reaction to seeing the number – a reaction which must have seemed crazy and extreme to the medical staff around me.

Seeing the new number – and realising what it actually represented – I couldn't help but chuckle. It was such a relief to realise that the true significance of the terrifying and all powerful G10 organisation was nothing more than my hospital room number. My shocked mind – existing as it had been in a comatose, unconscious state for over a year – had created a monster from something so simple and unthreatening as a number on a door.

"Glad to see you've got something to laugh about at last Michael" I looked to where the voice came from, saw Nurse Susan sitting on a chair beside my bed. I also noticed that I was no longer attached to any machines, medical drips or equipment of any sort – which was nice.

"Just a private joke" I quipped – you probably had to be there". I sat up, looked around the room – there were a couple of chairs, a small bedside table, a vase with some sort of flowers in and not much else. The window was large but too high to see through from the bed. I could see some sky – blue and cloudless. This made me feel happy and 'normal'.

I asked Susan if I was allowed out of bed and she said I could get out if I felt like it but to be careful as my leg muscles were very weak due to the lack of exercise one gets whilst lazing about in a coma.

I managed to stand – Susan supported me a little as I made my way towards the window. Outside it was bright and dry – there was a lovely car park extending into the distance and some wonderful office buildings and medical blocks all around. Cars moved around the perimeter roads, there were people shuffling about in a disorganised fashion.

"It's beautiful!" I quipped – not entirely joking. It was not the view itself of which I spoke but what that view represented – freedom – healing – normality – escape.

"You need to get out more Michael if you think that's lovely – there's a sewerage works down the road which you've just got to see – it'll blow your mind". We both laughed. Like normal people do in normal everyday life. It felt tremendous.

During the next few days I had to endure a lot of prodding, jabbing and medical assessment by various doctors. I made no complaints – I was too busy enjoying the feeling of normality – of being finally free of the mental nightmare – for that indeed was precisely what it had been. I began to regain strength in my body, my legs became capable of carrying me around without help. I ate and slept well.

I also spoke to a psychologist named Martha who listened keenly as I described some of the events my mind had experienced whilst my body had shut down completely. She seemed thrilled to get such a clear picture of what a coma patient had endured – it was quite rare it seemed, for someone to have such vivid and comprehensive memories in this situation. I felt a sense of relief as I finally got to expel the imaginary events to someone who wanted to listen. Part of me worried that this was just another level in the many layered imaginings of my coma landscape. I had had so many false awakenings. I didn't want this to be one of them. I had been convinced before. Had I really, finally, completely become conscious at last? Had all of the G10 brainwashing scenarios been no more than games played by my distressed or bored brain? My entering Art Mercer's garage a symbolic representation of my 'entering' the hospital as I became conscious of it?

After two weeks I was told that the medical staff felt I was strong enough both physically and mentally to have visitors. And so it was, a few days later that Johnny Walsh walked into my room with a big grin on his face.

"Ahoy old fella – nice to see you back in the land of the living". I felt a rush of chaotic emotion as he came closer to me. Much of the nightmare I had gone through was centred around this man – I had seen him decapitated, I had seen him arrange nuclear explosions, I had been manipulated by him many times – and now he was walking in as if nothing had happened. I realised of course that as far as his reality was concerned, nothing HAD happened – apart from I had been injured and in a coma – he was feeling relief and happiness at seeing me. I shook my confusion away – I'd had enough of it and preferred clarity and simplicity in my life from now on.

"Johnny, you old reprobate, how are you? Is that bloody Ford Anglia of yours on the road yet?"

"Of course it is – I don't know what you mean" he quipped. He sat on the chair next to my bed and beamed at me. "I'm really glad you're back to normal again Mike – or at least what passes for normal in your case".

"Thanks Johnny – it's very weird to see you again after all this time". It was too. I knew this was the real Johnny – my old Johnny – his character and personality shone out of him in a way that my mental construction of him never quite managed.

I got out of bed and we gave each other a hug – a thing we had never done before and would never do again. We were far too macho for that kind of thing. Then it was car talk – mechanical visions, greasy chat, parts numbers – the usual stuff we used to talk about. Johnny was not the kind of person to enquire about how I felt, my psychological state or any of that bollocks – he was a car guy and didn't intend to be anything else, for which I was extremely grateful.

We passed a very blokey couple of hours together – going along to the hospital canteen at one point to grab a coffee and some cakes – before he bade me a cheery goodbye and went off back to his latest mechanical project. I returned to my room, dozed for an hour or two, feeling delighted at how mundane my friend Johnny Walsh had remained.

I was soon able to think about moving out of the hospital – the medical staff were pleased with my progress and I was getting stronger each day – both physically and mentally. I had no idea what might have happened to my house – I had not been around to pay the mortgage for a while and there were not sufficient funds in my bank account to keep up the automatic Direct Debit payments for more than a few months – so maybe my house had been repossessed.

I asked about the belongings I'd had on me when I was first brought into hospital and was given a plastic bag which contained my keys, driving licence and a couple of bank cards. My sister Kirsty came to see me a few times during my convalescence and we chatted about not much – we'd never had much in common. I did mention to her my 'dream' or 'memory' about my visit to her when I'd had the police after me for the murder of Johnny Walsh – and she remembered nothing about it – because it hadn't actually happened. She laughed her head off, found it most amusing. I suppose it was from her side of the fence.

I was coming to terms with the fact that most of the things I remembered happening to me recently were just symptoms of my comatose state. The doctors recommended that I focus as much as possible on the person I used to be before the injury occurred – I could then use these true facts about myself as a firm basis for rebuilding my personality and life into something which would progress me beyond the trauma I had undergone – it would help me 'move on' as the trendy phrase would term it.

To this end, I called up my building society, spoke to them about my house. It had not yet been repossessed but was undergoing a legal process which would – unless action was taken on my part – inevitably lead to repossession. I explained my predicament and the manager of the building society said she would put a stop order on the procedure, write to me once a final decision and plan of action for repayment of arrears had been made. This was a positive start – I may be able to keep my home after all. I would need to get a job, but I felt confident in my ability to do so.

Three weeks later I was back in my little house in Winchester. It took a few days to get the dust and empty house smells out of it, to give it a thorough spring clean – even though it was autumn – the first it had ever had or was likely to have again.

I settled into a gentle routine – the psychologists had suggested it would help me acclimatise to reality more quickly. I got up at eight o'Clock each morning, had breakfast, went for a walk into the town centre, thereby getting some fresh air and exercise. After a few days I started to find this boring, so began to look for a job – I didn't intend to get one just yet – but I spent time seeing what was on offer, which wasn't much.

I had an urge to get involved in vehicle maintenance – maybe a job in a garage would suit. I was not really qualified for this as I had only really tinkered with vehicles – mainly motorcycles - had never shown any real ambition.

I liked the idea of buying old bikes, doing them up and selling them at a profit. It would mean I would not have a boss or be governed by someone else's timetable – I could work how and when it suited me. There was potentially a lot of money in it too – I had read *'Old Bike Mart'* for long enough to know how much interest there was in old bikes.

I received a compensation cheque for five grand, related to my injury, from some government department – it was an interim payment according to the letter which accompanied it. All the victims of the terrorist bomb were in line for a larger payout once a class action lawsuit on our behalf had cleared the court system – in a few months time, or so I had been informed. It was weird how things seemed to be panning out in much the same way as my last 'imagined' awakening. The mind was a very complex and mysterious piece of kit, that's for sure.

I began scouring the motorcycles magazines for a cheap bike and eventually settled on a rather sad looking – though mechanically fairly sound - Honda 250N Superdream – a classic bike which was now getting hard to find but which held a lot of happy memories for old bikers reliving their teens and twenties.

The bike cost me £1500, was delivered to me by the seller in an old battered pickup truck, which – like the motorcycle and its owner – had seen better days. I began to think of myself as a self-employed custom motorcycle restorer – it was a vast improvement on my previous view of myself – although I had a long way to go before I could really justify it. Someone once said – 'Fake it till you make it' – I decided to take this advice and had some cheap business cards printed with the name Garvie Custom Motorcycles on the front. I was back – and in business. Watch Out World!!

Chapter 17

It was as autumn ended and the first icy fingers of winter began to insinuate themselves into the landscape that I went out in my little boat *Beach Boy* for the first time since coming out of my coma. I had assumed my boat had been sold off and replaced by *Black Moon* – but that had been a false memory – *Beach Boy* was still moored in the harbour at Dover. My experience of it being sold had been nothing but overactive unconscious theatre – my invention of the *Black Moon* nothing more than a symbolic mental representation of my psyche's growing strength as I approached the waking point from my coma.

It felt odd, being back in a real boat after so many imaginary ones – and *Beach Boy* was a lot smaller than some of the other craft – *The Red Boat* and *Black Moon* – which I 'remembered' being on.

I felt a layer of tension creep over me as I gently eased the craft out of the docking area into the English Channel – so much of my nightmare had been linked to this stretch of water.

I didn't plan to stay out for long – just a little jaunt to keep me firmly on the path towards reclaiming my real life. I moved out as far as the three mile limit and dropped anchor. I made myself a ham sandwich and took my time over it, which improved the flavour somehow. I washed it down with a small glass of Captain Morgan Spiced rum, which I sipped as I watched birds in the clear blue sky and boats dotted about on the horizon.

I spent a few pleasant hours at sea before returning to shore and saying goodbye to my little boat. It helped me come to terms with the actual reality – that *Beach Boy* was still intact – and to accept that her demolition by Mark Hopkins had been nothing but a dream. I was finding it more difficult than expected to fully throw off the feeling that my life had been manipulated by a secret organisation – even when the facts were proving to me that this had not happened in reality.

There was an ominous feeling around me – or in my mind – that even though most of the facts themselves had been revealed – still a sense of some secret evil force being in control of my reality, lurking in the corners and shadows – was still present.

In an effort to get to the root of this problem, I decided to visit Johnny Walsh. I'd had time to think since his brief hospital visit and I wanted to talk to him about a few things which were troubling me – in particular, the thing which was troubling me most of all. Mark Hopkins.

Chapter 18

"Ahoy"

"Ahoy Johnny – it's your long lost pal Mike here – how's tricks shipmate?"

"Mike who?" Johnny replied – his sense of mischief was still strong. "I used to know a tosspot called Mike but he disappeared off the face of the earth"

"Well I'm back now dickhead so get the kettle on, I'm popping over this afternoon".

"I'll have to check my diary – see if its convenient" after a pause which lasted no longer than one quarter of a second he said "Yep, that's fine – I've made you an appointment for whenever you like"

"That's very gracious of you, you twat!"

"I thought so" We both laughed.

"See ya soon Johnny" I said before hanging up the phone.

I drove down to Johnny's place on my Honda 250N Superdream – I had spent a bit of time and money on the bike and it was purring like a kitten as I zoomed towards Southampton and out to Walsh's house.

As I pulled up I bipped my horn a few times – which brought back a few bad fake memories – pulled up right into his driveway, parking next to a very nicely restored and customised Ford Anglia – It could not possibly be the same heap he was working on last time I saw him – could it?

89

I took off my helmet, walked around the car – it had the same number plate so it must be the same vehicle – I was incredibly impressed with the improvements Johnny had made during my absence from the human race.

"Don't touch what you can't afford!" barked a voice behind me. I turned, saw Johnny Walsh – complete with head – holding out his hand and smiling at me. We shook hands, grinned at each other for a little while. His pride in the car was obvious and he could see that I was impressed.

"You've done an amazing job on this Anglia" was all I could think of to say.

"You're right there pal – It's a work of art – if I do say so myself".

"Can't argue with that, mate". Johnny beckoned me to follow him.

"Come in and have a cuppa – kettles on". He pointed to my Honda. "Nice little bike you've got there – couldn't you afford a proper one?"

"It's a classic – worth a lot these days"

"Just joshing Mike – I know these Superdream's are getting hard to get hold of these days – how much did it cost you?"

"£1500. Probably be able to sell it for at least £4000 now I've done it up"

"You probably could too mate – in fact I know a guy who has a small collection of 1970s Jap bikes – don't think he's got one of these"

"Maybe you could have a word with him".

"Probably could, yeah".

The kitchen was not as messy as I remembered – Johnny had obviously got his act together since I last saw him. He made two cups of strong tea, offered me a couple of Ginger Snaps –

which I took. We sat sipping our tea, the companionable silence we had shared for many years was still there as we made small talk about people we knew and had known.

When we had finished our drinks, we went back outside and Johnny proudly showed me his wonderful Ford Anglia – every nut and bolt of it – the man was obsessed.

"The new engine in this is a 3-litre V8 – goes like shit off a shovel – nought to sixty in just over 5 seconds".

"Fuck me – that is fast".

"I get a lot of satisfaction racing flash bastards in BMW's at the lights – you should see their shocked faces as I leave them in a pool of their own tears".

"Must be great".

"Oh, it is mate – maybe I'll take you for a little spin later – just into town and back – you can get a feel of the true power of the beast".

"Sounds like fun".

"It is. In fact why don't we go now – there's nothing stopping us".

So we did. It was a surreal experience driving around in an old car – yet overtaking every other vehicle we came across – Johnny must have left a lot of rubber on the roads that afternoon – I was terrified by some of his manoeuvres – but he was used to the power and control of the car, which was a minor miracle. The engine roared, purred and growled like a pride of lions and proved to be king of the jungle. Exhilarating is the only word for it.

"Well what do you think of the old crate Mike?" asked Johnny as we pulled up back in his driveway.

"Absolutely fantastic mate – you've done a superb job on it – can't believe it's the same car".

We went back inside, had a couple of beers, chewed the fat as the saying goes – then I left. Quite frankly I found the man boring beyond words.

Something had changed within my mind during my time of coma. I had experienced so much excitement and exhilaration – as well as fear and danger - that I could no longer feel a thrill from ordinary, everyday interactions and events.

I was beginning to feel that I had been cheated – not only by the injury I had sustained at the hands of the terrorists who had planted the bomb but by my life in general – I had been a nobody – a dull, unimaginative loser. My life had amounted to absolutely fucking zero. I was not willing to live out the rest of my existence in such a pointless fashion.

Although I had no specific plans for how my future would unfold, I knew for certain that I was going to add a lot of excitement to the mix.

I had almost completely moved on from my traumas, was ready to break out into something newer, more powerful, more real. There was just one thing I had to clarify – something which had been bugging me since I awoke from my unconscious dream state. I needed to find Mark Hopkins.

I had experienced many 'imagined' life and death scenarios involving this man but as far as I could remember, I had never met him in 'real' life – maybe he didn't even exist. Maybe it was just memory loss, or maybe he was just a figment of my imagination.

He had made an appearance at every level of my coma   nightmares and all of the 'false awakening scenarios' but was he simply a creation of my psyche? – some symbolic force of my personality which had never seen the light of day but which had taken the opportunity to assert itself whilst my control was down to nil. Was Mark Hopkins a real person? – or a repressed aspect of my own subconscious mind? It was time to find out.

Chapter 19

The English Channel was in a very bad mood as I piloted my little boat out of the harbour, into its angry vastness. *Beach Boy* rocked and rolled to such a degree that I had to hang on to the wheel to avoid being tossed into the sea. The forecast predicted that things would settle down before long and I had chosen to experience the tail end of its rage instead of waiting for the calm weather to arrive. I wanted to feel alive – and the best way to feel alive is to put your life into some degree of danger.

I was a little early, not really expecting things to pan out how I expected. I had decided to position myself on the direct route I would have taken if my 'experiences' of cigarette smuggling had been true.

A part of me thought maybe either a clone of myself – or the real me if I was the clone – or some other person – or Mark Hopkins himself – would be popping out into the channel to pick up the contraband in the exact manner and at the exact time and place I had 'imagined' in my coma. It was a crazy idea – borne of a desperate need to get to the bottom of this final mystery, but it had nagged away at me for so long I had decided to find out once and for all if any of my dreams had been based on truth.

So I waited until the time came for 'me' to turn up to collect the ciggies from the French boat piloted by the guy with the Leed's accent – the

Mysterious Lady – with which Mark Hopkins had rammed and destroyed the very boat I was now floating in – and which had been abandoned near Calais. It was crazy – I knew that – but I had to be sure so that I could move on to whatever future I had without the questions bothering me.

I waited for three hours – nothing happened. I moved position a few times – scanned the area for miles around. I went back towards the shore feeling like a fool. Even if the smuggling operation had been based on fact – it was more than likely that it may have been discontinued during my year away – or the personnel or timings would have been changed – I would have to cover the entire Channel continuously for months to get the full picture – and that was impossible.

Part of me was glad to abandon the plan – I didn't really want it to be true because that would get me wondering if other aspects or events of my coma dream had been true and I would end up being dragged into the whole mess again.

I moored my boat, raced home on the Honda in record – and highly illegal – time. I finished a Shepherds' Pie I had started two days ago, swigged a couple of Morgan's Spiced and went to bed early. I had to ride to Nottingham in the morning. I 'remembered' a time when I had stayed in a flat owned by Mark Hopkins – 12, Douglas Road - on the top floor if I remembered correctly.

It took me less than 2 hours to find the place. I recognised it, which was odd, considering I had supposedly only been here in a coma dream. I parked my bike, removed my crash helmet before entering the lobby and made my way up the stairs to the top floor. There was only one apartment on this level and the door was the same as I 'remembered' it. I approached the door cautiously and knocked. After only a few seconds the door opened – and there standing before me, smiling, was Mark Hopkins.

"Hello, Squirrel – long time no see" he said.

"Yep" was all I could say – I was in a state of shock. Mark's face took on a concerned look.

"You OK mate – you look like you've seen a ghost?" He beckoned me into the flat. I went in and sat on the sofa. "Want a drink? – rum is your poison of choice if I remember correctly".

"Thanks". He poured me a glass of Kraken spiced rum – it was a lot smoother than the Captain Morgan's I usually drank. It warmed my blood, enabled my mouth to work better. I told him I was fine as he sat down in an armchair facing me.

"Well I must say, you are about the last person I expected to see Mike".

"The feeling is mutual" I quipped.

"I heard you'd had some sort of bad accident, got injured in an explosion at Dover docks".

"A terrorist attack – a bomb went off and I got put in a coma for a year".

"Holy Shit!" Mark looked genuinely concerned. "I assume you're back to near normal now though Mate?"

I couldn't help but smile at his term 'near normal' - he was obviously still a witty bastard. But then why should he have changed if I had dreamt up all the traumatic, extreme activities we had – in my mind – shared recently.

"Near normal just about sums it up Mark" I replied.

"I had to stop the fag run after you disappeared – there were a lot of police and army hanging around Dover for quite a while after the incident. I didn't fancy being noticed hanging around there".

"Makes sense – so you're no longer smuggling cigarettes in from France then?"

"Not at the moment. Mind you it was a good little earner – I don't suppose you'd like to get back into that line of work – we both made a nice bit of dosh out of it didn't we?".

"No – you're alright – I'm trying to stay on the straight and narrow for the time being Mark".

"Same here" he said.

"So what you doing now to make a crust?" I enquired.

"A bit of this, bit of that". He laughed. "Actually I'm in the property game – I buy and sell a few properties – it keeps the wolf from the door. I don't suppose you want to buy this place do you – I've been living here for a few years and I'm looking to move out of Nottingham – maybe a house in the country".

"Thanks for the offer Mark but I'm fine where I am for the present – still in my poky little two bed semi in Winchester".

"Well if you ever want to sell it and move, give me a bell – I've got quite a few contacts in the property game now Mate".

"I'll bear that in mind".

We chatted about nothing of great import for another hour or so before I made my excuses and left. I had a feeling he was as bored with the whole conversation as I was.

I could strike Mark Hopkins off of my list of supervillains once and for all. It was a relief.

I had now satisfied myself as to the veracity of the 'Coma Narrative' – I believed it was genuine. I had checked it out and found it not inconsistent with reality. It was true that I had actually been involved with Mark Hopkins in a cigarette smuggling operation but I would have been surprised if nothing whatever of my real life had infiltrated the coma dream-state. Imaginings have to be built on something – I had created events and experiences involving Mark Hopkins which had blown his character out of all proportion to the real man – who was rather dull in my opinion. Maybe that was why I had forgotten having met him before. Some actual memory damage had obviously occurred. If I had remembered things which hadn't happened, it was just as likely that I would have forgotten some things which had happened.

I was finding everybody exceedingly dull – my life was dull, the human race was dull. Dull. Dull. Dull.

Chapter 20

I sold the Honda for a profit of £2000 a few days later. I decided not to continue with my motorcycle restoration business. I found it too mundane. I needed something more stimulating. I was extremely uninspired by the options I saw before me.

I had received a further £40,000 in compensation after the court case was settled in favour of the victims – so I was free to pursue a new path in life. My problem was that I couldn't think of a single option which inspired me.

I toyed with the idea of writing a novel based upon the events I had experienced whilst in the coma but decided it was too far-fetched to be believable.

I drifted aimlessly – made a few visits to places I hadn't been before – Liverpool, Maidenhead, Bodmin, - random places which did nothing to assuage my growing need for something more meaningful. I started to drink too much, smoke too much – I was back on them – eat too much.

I was frustrated and depressed. Life could offer nothing to me. At least 'normal' life could not. I considered other options. Immoral, illegal options. Here I found a thrill – a sense of joy almost. I decided to work outside the norms of society – in short I chose to become a criminal. It felt good.

My first crime would be to smuggle cigarettes from France to England in my boat – I would buy them cheap in Calais and sell them to somebody here in England – maybe I could get Mark Hopkins involved in the operation again – this time with me as the top dog and him as one of my underlings. Yes, that sounded a good idea – it could work and it would certainly be thrilling to try.

I would start small – after all I wasn't in it for the money I was in it for the thrill of breaking the law, the hope of getting away with it. Even getting a carton of 200 fags into the country without paying the duty on them would give me a sense of victory over this dull world and its pointless rules. I would become a pirate, a renegade, a maverick. I would laugh in the face of officialdom – break their stupid rules and get away with murder. Literally.

To this end I took my little boat *Beach Boy* – across the Channel once more. I moored in the harbour at Calais. I took a local bus to the nearest hypermarché, bought a box of 1000 cigarettes. Then I went back to my boat and calmly sailed back to England. I had been in and out of the harbour at Dover many times, had never been challenged by customs officials. This time was no different. I decided to add to my excitement and risk by visiting the White Cliffs pub.

I went inside, ordered a pint of lager and a rum chaser. Dermot Leach served me in a friendly manner but other than that didn't seem to recognise me. I beckoned him aside and we went into the quieter side of the pub – a smaller bar with more tables and less customers – mainly used to serve food.

"I don't know if you remember me – I'm a friend of Mark Hopkins" I said. I couldn't actually remember if Dermot knew Mark or if it had been part of my coma dream – I was past caring what was real, what was not and how it all fitted together. At the end of the day it was my actions which counted - not thoughts, imaginings or understandings – I *was* my behaviour. That is all I was – you could keep the explanations and you could shove the truth up your jacksy as far as I was concerned – it had proved nothing but trouble.

Dermot made a face. "I don't know any Mark Hopkins".

"Don't worry about it mate. I've got a little proposition for you".

"Oh yeah?" he sounded cautious. I can't say I blamed him – I was acting rather oddly – I knew that – but the thrill of illicit behaviour had me in its grip and I enjoyed his confusion.

"I've just popped over to France to buy some fags and I bought a few too many – I just wondered if you'd like to buy some off me – at a discount obviously".

"25% off the retail price would get me interested" he replied.

"I can do 20%" I responded. He thought about it for all of five seconds before agreeing to the deal.

"I'll write you a cheque – what name is it?"

"Leave it out pal – d'you think I'm stupid?"

"No, just testing" he laughed at my discomfort – he had been winding me up. He passed me a small pile of notes and I handed over the box of fags.

"Nice to do business with you   sorry I don't know your name..."

101

"Call me Mark"

"Dermot"

We shook hands. "Might be able to get a few more if you're interested"

"Sure – why not". I left feeling great. I had pulled off my first crime. It had been easy. I looked forward to my next one. It would have to be on a bigger scale. Maybe if I could *steal* a box of cigarettes I could make a much bigger profit next time.

After giving it a little thought I decided not to risk my own arse stealing cigarettes. Instead I found a weasely little worm to do it for me. His name was Gez, short for Gerald. I met him through Dermot Leach after we had traded a few times and he had decided he could trust me. He was wrong about that but it would be his problem not mine. Gez had a knack for breaking into supermarkets, nicking large amounts of fags when no-one was looking. I paid him about 20% of what they were worth but I offered him a quick turnaround, no need to hang on to the goods after he had acquired them – therefore limiting his risk of getting caught and guaranteeing him some quick money. The arrangement worked well. I sold the cigs on to Dermot at a 40% markup and he made a further 40% when he sold them to his growing customer base.

After a few months of this, Gez was struggling to keep up with the orders we requested and brought another man - an equally weasely cousin named Billy Dashwood – who helped to increase our supply of contraband somewhat. It was not enough – we were increasing our buyers too quickly – supplies were running short from time to time. We needed a bigger operation.

Dermot and I decided it would be even more lucrative if we could also get hold of stolen booze – many contacts he had in the trade would ensure a ready supply of customers for alcohol. We would make a fortune.

We asked Gez if he could get us some bottles of rum, whisky, vodka to go along with the fags he supplied. He was not keen – saying he couldn't cope with the quantities of cigarettes we were asking for – let alone bottles of spirits – he would need at least five men and a couple of lorries to pull it off.

He was also concerned that his increased activities were already coming to the notice of the police – he had been questioned by two different police forces recently and was not willing to risk being banged up. He wanted to give it a rest for a while, let things die down. From his perspective it made total sense. From my perspective it sounded like I needed to replace him with someone with more backbone and ambition.

I went to Nottingham, discussed the opportunity with Mark Hopkins. He was cautious at first but became more interested when I told him how much money I was making. I knew he had a lot of contacts in the smuggling trade – he was probably still involved in it – he just thought that maybe I had become a liability to him after my coma – that's how I interpreted his attitude when I last visited him. He had closed me out of his little gang. Now I was asking him to put his gang at my disposal and move into stolen goods rather than just avoiding customs duty and tax on products he brought in from France.

I told him about the involvement of Dermot Leach – a man he didn't know in reality but who had been one of his main cronies in my coma dream. That was a bit weird – I was finding it harder to remember which memories were true and which imaginary – but it didn't seem to matter that much in actuality.

He knew a couple of people who would be willing and able to steal a lot of booze from certain warehouses in the Nottingham area – he had toyed with the idea of raiding the places himself but had lacked the customer base to offload the goods quickly enough, so had refrained from putting his plans into action. I had the contacts to offload the contraband if he had the contacts to pilfer the stuff in the first place. It was a perfect fit. I would pay him 30% of the retail price of the goods he supplied – out of which he would pay his thieves their cut. I would sell the goods on to my contacts for 60% of the retail price – giving them 40% - which had to be shared with whoever they sold the stuff to. It was a good deal – everyone got a fair percentage.

I was very pleased with my cut – I was basically buying bent gear from Hopkins and selling it to my main buyers – I didn't have to do much at all – I was a middleman – it suited me. Hopkins was in a similar situation – he bought the stuff from his thieves and sold them to me – he also had to do very little – we were the big fish and we liked it. We took less risk for our money – the people at each end of the chain were in considerably more danger than we were – much more likely to get busted.

Mark and I shook hands on the deal. Smiles all round.

It took a few weeks to get the necessary arrangements and personnel in place. I received the first shipment from Mark on a rainy Saturday night. A lorry load of alcohol and cigarettes – lifted from a warehouse in Nottingham the night before. I drove it to Dover and offloaded it into Dermot's cellar around noon the next day – we unloaded in broad daylight – it looked like a normal delivery to a public house – what could be less suspicious?

The amount of money I was making was increasing on a week by week basis – by the end of the summer I had over £250,000 in my bank account. I bought a nice detached house in Dover – I was spending more time there now – mainly aboard my boat or at the White Cliffs pub. Dermot too was making a good living, selling a lot of stolen fags and booze to his growing customer base. The place was buzzing. Dermot was a happy man. He now had enough income to send various donations to his political cronies – who shall remain nameless.

Mark Hopkins had sold his Nottingham apartment and like me, had moved to Dover. He paid cash for a luxury apartment in the city centre.

The organisation – which I had named 'Black Moon Ltd' had been registered at Companies House and described as a wholesaler and retailer of 'general goods'. We planned to keep enough of our trades legit – so it would not look suspicious if Mark and I started buying properties and flash motors – the tax man would get a fair cut of our legal business but hopefully would not become aware of our really lucrative criminal activities.

105

I was the Chairman and Managing director of the company – Mark was a director. A few months in we got Johnny Walsh onto the board as a non-executive director – a silent partner – not long after that we brought in Art Mercer too. We were expanding into dodgy motor parts now and Art in particular was setting up a lot of lucrative contacts on that side of the business. We were all having a wonderful time and I was feeling more alive than ever before – I hadn't realised just how enjoyable organised crime could be.

Chapter 21

I decided I needed a bigger boat, so I looked around marinas and studied the For Sale ads in boating magazines until I found what I was looking for – a Westsail 32.

I found one – it was moored in Falmouth, Cornwall and was in fully restored condition – the interior had recently been upgraded and was immaculate. The price was high but I could easily afford it and bought it without quibbling over the price. I arranged to have it brought to Dover. It arrived by sea a few weeks later. It looked really good, moored next to *Beach Boy*.

It is supposedly 'bad luck' to change the name of a boat but I had stopped believing in such superstitions – I changed her old name – *Marguerite,* to *Black Moon.* I also had her keel painted black and the latest navigational equipment installed.

I sailed around the Channel for a bit, found her to be a strong, comfortable craft – identical to the one I had dreamed up in my coma holiday.

I was aware that I had been acting a little out of character lately, had become obsessed with enacting or recreating elements of my imagined past in my present. It didn't really bother me, although I did wonder if it was entirely healthy.

Life before my injury had been dull and mediocre – I was nobody going nowhere – now I was at least living life more fully – it was exciting and lucrative – a definite improvement.

My colleagues in crime were not aware of my acting out of coma elements, as I had not gone into any detail, regarding the experiences I had undergone.

I had some minor interactions with police from time to time – as did the others involved. One of our vans had been seen near the scene of a warehouse raid in Kent but it was one of several vehicles passing by – so no real threat to our existence. There was another incident involving Johnny Walsh which came to nothing but looked a bit dodgy at the time. His fingerprints had been found inside a warehouse in Bedfordshire, which had been robbed. He could not adequately account for this, so the cops pulled him in for questioning. I was surprised to find out that they even had his dabs on file. As far as I knew – and Johnny had never told me any different – he had never been in trouble with the police before.

It turned out that he had once been officially cautioned for being drunk and disorderly, had been obliged to give his fingerprints to the police at that time.

When questioned regarding his prints being found inside the warehouse he just played dumb – said he couldn't account for them being there and was surprised to hear, from the police, that they were indeed there. It was not a crime for your fingerprints to appear at the scene of a crime and Johnny considered it more than likely that there were about a hundred sets of prints, made by all kinds of innocent people found in the same location. It was possible that the accuracy of the fingerprint boys was not all it was cracked up to be. Either way the cops had bugger all to go on and moved on to other lines of enquiry.

We knew that as things stood we were probably still in the clear regarding actual suspicion from the police but that records would be kept of every interaction between them and our criminal gang members. The police would be quick to spot any patterns which might emerge within such fields of general enquiry – if the same names kept 'innocently' popping up, it would begin to look less innocent. We didn't want to get onto actual 'suspect' lists.

In order for things to blow over regarding the warehouse jobs – which were getting rather numerous and becoming a high priority for the cops – we decided to put our activities on hold for a couple of months. Everyone involved would have made enough profit out of previous ventures to last a few weeks without extra income. We had always planned to let things cool down at intervals – let the trail go cold and the fuzz lose interest before starting up again.

A call went out to everyone involved that they were to cool it for a while – until given the green light to begin again. The only people who were unhappy about this were the end users of our contraband products – they had to start paying full price for their fags and booze for a while – although many of them had built up stockpiles which would keep them going for months – if not years.

We used this time to take holidays – rest, recuperate – and come up with new, even more grandiose plans for future expansion and profit within the Black Moon crime syndicate.

One area we decided to develop was the stolen car market. Art mercer had been selling more nicked car parts and along with Johnny Walsh, had managed to make contact with some fairly important faces running an international stolen car ring. They were headquartered in Italy but were mainly English guys who had set up out there to facilitate ease of transportation to the North African and Middle Eastern buyers of most of the cars.

They concentrated on luxury vehicles, could have a newly acquired Mercedes or BMW shipped to a customer in Morocco or Saudi Arabia within days. New number plates, documents and paint jobs were taken care of in Wolverhampton. Johnny had set up a highly efficient 'transformation hub', staffed by highly skilled specialists. Art organised the transportation of the adapted vehicles to the continent and the people in Naples did the rest. It all ran smoothly for a few months.

I had not until later, realised how advanced – and lucrative - Johnny and Art's car activities had become. Mark Hopkins didn't seem to know much about it either – he was annoyed when I let him know what I had discovered. There developed a feeling that Art and Johnny were attempting to cut the rest of us out of the picture to some degree.

When we raised this issue at our next syndicate meeting – held at the White Cliffs pub in Dover – Johnny just shrugged like we were making a mountain out of a mole hill.

"I can't see what your problem is lads" he smirked "We all have our own way of making a few quid"

"Yes, but we are supposed to be working as a team – not just covering our own asses and lining our own pockets" Mark countered.

"All our profits go into the Black Moon coffers mate – just like the profits you make". I wondered if this was actually true – I had not looked into the income streams on the accounts for some time – I would have to make an appointment with Adam Lester – our highly creative accountant - a man who ran two sets of books – one for Her Majesty's Revenue and Customs – and one which detailed all our illegal transactions, which Adam kept stowed away in some deep dark recess, only he knew the exact location of.

"Feel free to check with Adam if you have any concerns" it was as if Johnny could read my mind.

"I'm due to see him in a few days – I'm sure everything is above board. We will all gain from sticking together – an organisation is only as strong as its weakest link".

"Quite right Mike – I couldn't agree more". Johnny's voice was laced with a smugness I didn't like. I would make sure to have a really good look at those books.

Mark Hopkins didn't look any too happy. He glowered at Johnny in a way which would have unsettled most people. Johnny just smirked at him and the meeting broke up in a not too friendly way. It was the first time we had felt any conflict between members of the board of directors of Black Moon Ltd.

I could sense future problems developing if I didn't take action to protect myself and what I saw as MY organisation – I had started the company and the organised crime syndicate behind it. I

111

would not let petty squabbles or greedy bastards wreck what I had achieved.

From that moment on I saw all of my colleagues as potential weak points – perhaps even problems to be taken into account. I was determined that I should gain control of as many elements of the organisations activities as possible.

I spent the next couple of months reinforcing and strengthening my position. I made arrangements to meet with Adam Lester on a monthly basis. I found the books to be more or less what I expected – though the profits entered from the stolen car racket run by Johnny and Art were slightly lower than I had expected. I would need to keep an eye on the pair of them. If they thought they could rip me off they were mistaken. I made an arrangement with Adam, whereby he told me where he kept the books in return for a large increase in salary – not to go on the books – a little secret between us. He had a second, smaller office in Switzerland where he kept his most important files and accounts. I was given a key to the office and the combination of the safe – it cost me a lot of money but was an important part of my plan.

I visited him in Geneva, took a look around the area and the office itself. The combination I had been given – like the keys – were legit. Adam had been honest with me. He went on my very short 'People I Can Probably Trust' list. It was very short indeed. I was thinking of scrapping it altogether. I could see no benefit from trusting anyone.

While I was in Geneva I procured one of those world famous numbered Swiss Bank Accounts. It was not necessary to give any of my details – not even my name. As long as I had the number I could access the account and the large safe deposit box linked to the account.

I transferred half a million pounds cash into this account, placed the keys, the safe combination details relating to Adam's office, along with a few thousand pounds worth of gold bullion, in the deposit box.

I waited for Adam to fly back to England before returning to his Swiss office and getting myself a copy of the latest accounts. I would return from time to time to acquire updates. If anything happened to Adam I wanted to be sure to have access to the figures.

I was satisfied with the financial side of things – my 'legal' income from legitimate business transactions was now high enough for me to buy a flash motor without drawing suspicion from the Inland Revenue – or even worse, the police.

I decided it was time to buy a Porsche - I was not a 'boy racer' so I avoided the usual 'Jack-the-Lad' models and went for a deep red Panamera with matching red alloy wheels. This was a 4-door saloon – quite a new venture for Porsche – and had all the style and a lot more class than the ones the stockbrokers were racing around in. I wanted to project an image of class and wealth – not make myself look like a complete tosspot.

I had to wait six weeks for the car to arrive. It turned up on the back of a transporter and was unloaded onto the nice gravel driveway of my big house in Dover. I felt like a king. I had come a long way since my rebirth. My life was segmented into two parts – 'Before' and 'After' my life-changing coma.

I spent a week driving around in my new car and sailing my sleek new boat around the coast. It was idyllic. I drank copious amounts of Captain Morgan's Spiced Rum, smoked a highly dangerous amount of cigarettes – I was on the Gitanes now – and ate nothing but ham sandwiches, which I sledge-hammered down my throat in fanatical succession. I was on a celebratory binge – the like of which had never been seen before.

I made myself ill and became weak. I coughed a lot, felt like my stomach was about to burst – I put on half a Stone in a week and had the worst hangover I'd ever experienced. On the plus side, I released a lot of built up tension and frustration. I had also indulged my growing need to acknowledge my 'old self'. I was still the boy I used to be. I may be living a different life but I would never again forget the person I had been for all of those years. I was still Michael Garvie.

Soon, the warehouse robberies were back on – although we changed the areas of operation – moved up north where our activities would not be recognised as part of an ever-widening series of warehouse robberies – just single unconnected incidents – or so we hoped. I was not so naïve as to think the police wouldn't catch on sooner or later. People would be pulled in for questioning, some even charged. It was then that we would find out if anyone was going to grass on their mates to save their own skin. I would need to make some sort of contingency plan to keep myself out of the frame if things got a bit dicey.

I contacted a man I had heard about through various underworld contacts I had built up as the organisation grew. He ran a security firm in Bristol –

some said it was linked to protection rackets across the country. I wanted to meet him personally, decide what sort of person he was. I would only let him in on my plans if he convinced me he was worthy of my 'People I Can Probably Trust' list.

I drove to Bristol in my Panamera, parked outside a rough-looking industrial complex near the river Avon. I had arranged to meet Paul Nixon at 11am inside the foyer of the Ardent Security Services Ltd, headquarters – which sounded a lot more impressive than it looked. I was punctual. Paul was there waiting for me. We shook hands and I followed him down a greasy grey corridor into his office.

Inside, it was a lot smarter than I had been led to expect – judging from the general run-down grimness of the outer facade of the buildings.

"This is nice" I quipped.

"Yes isn't it? A lot better than you expected"

"True"

"We keep the place looking dilapidated – it keeps nosy parkers at bay – not to mention the Tax bastards"

"I imagine it would at that" I joked. He smiled, offered me a drink. I chose a single malt Scotch – on the rocks. Paul's office was well appointed – fridge stocked with cold beers, food. Fancy Chesterfield sofa against the wall. Television monitor screen, some high class radio equipment and other electronic gubbins which I could not recognise.

We settled down amongst the luxury, sipping our drinks and sizing each other up for a couple of minutes.

"I understand you are looking for some customised security services?" he declared.

"That's one way of putting it, I suppose, Paul" I chuckled.

"What exactly did you have in mind? I can assure you that this room is secure and you need not concern yourself with privacy issues. I have built my business on my reputation for complete trustworthiness".

"Nice to know". I replied.

"Whatever you want, we can provide – I assure you" There was something about the way he said this which made me uncomfortable – I knew I was in the presence of a man who would not be limited by legalities – or moralities - if the situation required extreme action. I had been told by my contact that Ardent Security were willing to take out contracts of a specialist nature - and by contracts, he meant 'contracts'.

"Well, initially I just want some of my employees – and fellow directors – kept an eye on, if you know what I mean?"

"Certainly. We can watch and report on any amount of people – our reports to include video or other hard evidence which might seem relevant or crucial. Is that the sort of thing you're looking for Mr. Garvie?".

"Exactly that" I replied.

"Then we can do business" he said. We shook hands on it. I gave him certain information and he informed me that regular reports would reach me at my home address on a frequent basis. I wrote him out a cheque for £15,000 – his services were not cheap. Who the hell wants cheap security?

I would be paying a similar amount to him every month whilst I used his services. If I required 'other projects' undertaken I would pay whatever the going rate was at the time on an Ad Hoc basis.

I drove home to Dover, arrived around midnight. I had a shower, a drink and went to bed. I slept more soundly than I had for a long time. My sense of control over my company – and my life – had been strengthened considerably and it felt great.

Chapter 22

The stolen car racket started slowly but expanded rapidly. Johnny and Art were good at what they did and the Italians were experts at shifting the cars once they'd had their identities and paperwork altered.

Their highly professional approach suggested links to the Italian Mafia. I called Paul Nixon, asked him to look into it for me. I received a report from him ten days later – along with a hefty bill.

The Italians who customised and re-documented the stolen cars were not part of the Mafia – though some of them did associate with Mafia members – mainly on a social level. This was normal according to Paul – it is virtually impossible to be involved in organised crime in Italy without at least some casual links to the Cosa Nostra. The report stated that there was currently no significant interest in our set up from the Mob.

There had, however been an increasing amount of contact – mainly social – between a Mafia middleman and Johnny Walsh. It seemed that this middleman, named Julio Montefiore, had been holding cosy little chats with Johnny – and to a lesser extent Art Mercer – who visited the Italian garages far less often than Johnny, preferring to stay local to his home base.

The report suggested I have Ardent Security operatives monitor the situation on an ongoing basis and report any significant changes or activities. I phoned Paul, thanked him for his report, asked him to continue with low-level surveillance.

Things ran smoothly for the next six months. All of our operations brought in huge profits. My Swiss bank account expanded exponentially. I became rich. A millionaire in fact. I began to consider what I should do with the money – it seemed pointless just having it sit in a bank, doing nothing.

I already had a big house and a fancy motor. I was satisfied with my boat – *Black Moon* – she wasn't a large yacht – there were boats so big you could keep other boats inside them, but she was all I required. I wasn't a womaniser, a gambler or a drug addict – if I had been, I would have spent a lot more cash.

I didn't waste my money, I let it gain interest; made a few sensible investments; generally let my wealthy life plod forward in the luxurious manner I was becoming used to – and maybe slightly bored with.

My need for excitement – which had developed since my injury and coma – was making itself felt again. I had managed to satisfy my urges for some time with the build up of my criminal activities and my company, Black Moon Ltd.

The legitimate side of the business – mainly buying and selling car parts and various bulk goods, which were sold to honest shop keepers and dealers – was making a good profit. Not the sort of money the illegal side of my activities was bringing in – but decent growth.

I paid an increasing amount of tax and VAT to the Revenue & Customs department and they were happy to get it. I was a success in the eyes of the world – and the underworld. But the sense of ease which my success brought me began to cause frustration in my mind. I needed something with an element of danger and excitement in order to feel more alive.

I went to see Mark Hopkins. I had not visited him since he moved into his luxury apartment in Dover. We had met at the crime syndicate meetings and company board meetings – but I had not been out to his home and I fancied having a butchers at his set up. You can tell a lot about a man by how he lives.

His flat was spacious, with a lot of nice paintings on the walls – mainly landscapes by Turner and Constable – worth a lot of money if genuine.

"I like what you've done with the place"

"It suits my refined tastes" he replied with a smug grin.

"You should buy a country manor, set yourself up as the local squire".

"You never know mate – I have been thinking along those lines myself recently – might be fun".

"Just think of all those scullery maids and serving wenches you'd need to employ".

"I have been. I'd obviously need a helicopter to get back into the city when required – and maybe a chauffeur driven limo for important social functions"

"Of course"

We sat on plush, expensive sofas, sipping classy drinks from crystal glasses. The carpet was deep enough to hide a kitten in the pile. It was obvious that Mark was living life to the full. I could see him retiring in a couple of years – maybe to a stately home surrounded by acres of woodland. He would walk around his estate wearing a monocle, carrying a Purdey shotgun with which to shoot pheasants – and poachers.

He would probably take less interest in the business as his enjoyment of the quiet, wealthy life expanded. I envied him. My future was not to be so cosy – my desperate need for thrills would not enable me to follow a similar path towards a contented old age.

I could, however, benefit from Mark's desire to enjoy wallowing in luxury – he might be open to a suggestion from me to sell some or all of his shares in Black Moon Ltd. I was already the largest shareholder in the company with over 40% of the shares – but if I could get another 11% I would gain total control over the business. I wanted control – as much of it as I could get. Things were looking interesting.

I visited Art Mercer the following week. He was still the same old Art – overalls and grease. He had cleared out some of the old cluttered space, which had previously been filled with knackered old boat engines and other general odds & sods. In place of the junk was a new warehouse racking system – it looked a lot more professional. On the new shelves were car parts and accessories - neatly arranged, boxed and labelled. This was the central hub of the legitimate business of Black Moon Ltd. Art had lost interest in the shadier side of operations, seemed happy to keep the genuine trade ticking over.

This suited me. I welcomed the stability of the honest side of the business: the higher the profits from Art's endeavours, the more I would be justified in spending on things I liked. I made sure all my dodgy cash went straight into my Swiss account. My earnings from the straight company dealings could be paraded in front of the tax man with no worries about it looking shifty. Art was a definite benefit to me.

I was satisfied with the way things were progressing with Mark and Art.

I needed to check out Johnny Walsh. I decided to visit him in a few days' time. He was spending an increasing amount of time in Naples – involved in the bent car racket but He still owned his old house in the New Forest and it was there that I arranged to meet him.

I had received an update from Paul Nixon at Ardent Security Ltd a day earlier. His agents had found Johnny even more involved with the Mafia – especially Julio Montefiore. It was now believed – although no absolute proof had yet been obtained – that Johnny was syphoning off a percentage of the profits into his own bank account, was taking part in mafia funded projects which cut me out of the deal altogether. The report suggested he was about to go all in with the Mob and effectively steal the whole Italian end of the car racket, placing it in the hands of the Cosa Nostra. Whether this was due to duress, persuasion or plain greed was not yet known. I gave Ardent the permission – and the funding – to go full bore into their investigation of Johnny Walsh.

I spoke to Paul Nixon personally a few times, concerning this and other matters. We built a rapport – based upon a similar general outlook on how things should be run. Paul was very ambitious to extend the sphere of operations of Ardent but currently lacked the funds to do so. I suggested that I buy into the company and get a seat on the board. He agreed. The deal was done. I put two million into the company in return for a 51% stake and a seat on the board. I was now the controlling stakeholder – in effect the company was mine – to do with as I pleased. I trusted Paul, respected his knowledge of the industry and his highly professional approach to the job, so I let him remain managing Director – upped his salary – and left him a happy man.

There was only one change I insisted upon before we expanded into certain other professional areas of business. I had the name of the company changed. 'G10 Security Ltd' was open for business. I did not feel the need to notify any of my colleagues about these changes.

Johnny Walsh was a changed man. Gone were the old mechanics overalls, gone the clutters of junk – gone even the once-beloved Ford Anglia. Gone the man I once knew.

The new Johnny dressed in flashy Italian suits, wore sunglasses indoors and was as slippery as an eel. It was hard to accept that a person could change so fundamentally in such a short space of time.

His house – once scruffy but homely – was now half empty – it looked like he was in the process of moving out.

"Wow, Johnny – things have certainly changed around here mate"

"We all have to move with the times Michael" he replied.

We sat at the kitchen table – he didn't offer me a cuppa or anything stronger – it felt like he didn't really want me here at all, couldn't wait to get rid of me. I decided to forgo the usual pleasantries and cut to the chase.

"I've been hearing some rumours that you are getting involved with the Mob in Italy Johnny – any truth to them?"

"Depends what you mean by 'involved'" he quipped – a smirk edging across his face.

"I mean that maybe you are cutting your old mates out of the car racket, giving our profits to your new pals, the Mafia"

"Depends what you mean by 'cutting out'" he grinned.

"What I mean is you are stealing our business and trying to take over the operation. What I mean is you are keeping profits for yourself instead of passing them into our agreed bank accounts. What I mean is you are getting far too pally with your new chum Julio Montefiore. What I mean is you have turned into a right fucking arsehole. What I mean is you are walking on very fucking thin ice pal. What I mean is you have one month to get back in line or I will be forced to take remedial action. I hope I have made myself clear enough for you to understand Johnny".

I hadn't meant to lose my rag but I just could not stand smug smirky bastards. Johnny just grinned even wider.

"Thanks for stating your position so clearly Mike". He spat out the 'Mike' like it was an insult or a swear word. "Now let me clarify a few things for you. Firstly – yes you are correct in surmising that I am doing a bit of business with Julio and his associates – I will be doing all of my business with them sooner than you expect. Secondly, I do not care what small time chancers like you and Art mercer think – because you are small fry and of no consequence whatever as far as I am concerned. Thirdly – and this is the clincher – there is absolutely nothing you can do about it – our plans are already activated 'pal'. The car racket is lost – my new colleagues have, as of just this morning, moved in and taken over the whole of the Italian side of the business. The English side is no longer of any consequence. We have moved the staff from the Wolverhampton hub to Naples. Without the ability to alter the cars and get new documents done, you are stuck with a lot of hot motors which cannot be shifted out of the country because *we* control that country – you'll just have to keep hold of them, hope you can sell them before the police find them. I have a suspicion that that event might also be closer than you could possibly imagine".

"You mean you've informed the police?" I barked. "You'll be pulled in too – you have been the main person behind the car stealing – you're crazy if you think they won't have a warrant out for your arrest.

"Cool your jets pal – I'm just toying with you – we don't need to call the cops in – your operation is nothing – without the Italian side – its going nowhere".

"We'll see about that Johnny".

"Yes we will Michael". We stood facing each other. Me snarling through gritted teeth – him grinning in wrap-around shades. I turned and walked slowly towards the door.

"Enjoy the rest of your life Johnny. You are no longer part of Black Moon – you are out of the operation."

"I already was out – you just didn't know it".

"You're finished" I growled.

"I'm just getting started Garvie!"

"That's what you think".

I stormed out, drove back home in a foul mood. If Walsh thought he could rip me off and get away with it he had another think coming. How far his plans – or more likely the mafia's plans - to take over the stolen car operation had progressed I didn't know. I had heard little more than rumours of cosy meetings from Paul Nixon's security guys and I wondered if Johnny was just acting the big shot due to nothing more than an overblown ego. It was possible. If this was the case, he had made a big mistake – alerting me to the future plans he and his new cronies were preparing to undertake.

I phoned Paul as soon as I got home. He answered on the second ring.

"Michael, I'm glad you called – I need to speak to you urgently about our little Italian problem".

"What about it?"

"It's about to become a big problem".

"Yeah, I'm ahead of you Paul". I tried to keep the slight edge of sarcasm out of my voice but a bit of it stayed in. I was a little unimpressed that I was paying Nixon a lot of money to let me know things I already knew.

"I doubt it Michael. I have been informed – literally an hour ago – that Julio Montefiore and a couple of his gang are flying over to England to visit Johnny Walsh later today. My agent has been working inside the local Mob for a few months now – not a high position but one from which some good information has come. He has been employed as Nicola Gennari's chauffeur and managed to overhear some snippets of conversation between Gennari and Montefiore."

"Who is Gennari?"

"He's the younger son of Antonio Gennari – the head of the Naples family. He is slowly replacing Antonio, who is in his seventies and prefers golf to extortion these days."

"What's he been saying to Julio?" I asked.

"From what I can gather, Julio has been given the green light to make a move on a new operation which concerns Johnny Walsh and the car racket"

"Old news Paul!" I countered. "I saw Walsh not two hours ago and he couldn't wait to inform me that they were taking over the whole racket – and the English operation is nothing without the Italian – that's what he told me. Are you saying it's true?".

"Yes Michael – it's true. The contract will be signed with Walsh later today – tomorrow they move – and move big!"

"What can we do to stop them?" I asked, already knowing the answer.

"Not a lot actually. We don't have enough power in Italy to hold on to the business – the local Italians will change sides if the Mob tells them to."

"And without them we will be stuck with a lot of hot cars we can't get rid of! Johnny's already pointed that out to me".

"That's about the size of it". Paul sounded disappointed. Angry and disappointed.

Two hours later I met Paul at the Dover Heliport – the flight had saved many hours driving.

127

Paul was relaxed. Relaxed and determined. We were not finished by a long chalk. We hadn't even started!

Chapter 23

The morning radio news carried an item about a violent murder which had taken place overnight. A suspected criminal had been shot and killed by a known member of the Italian Mafia. His head had been blown off with a shotgun. The shotgun had been found by police in the boot of the killer's car. Two other men who had been travelling in convoy in a second car had also been detained for questioning.

I received a phone call just after I got up for breakfast.

A voice said "Job Done".

I smiled briefly. Then I had a plate of bacon and eggs, followed by a nice cup of tea.

Later that day I phoned Art Mercer, asked him if he had heard the news. He had. He sounded slightly more relaxed than before. I also phoned Mark Hopkins – he was ecstatic. We all agreed that an irritant – a unnecessary complication – had been removed from our lives.

Some adjustments were made regarding share ownership of Black Moon Ltd. There were clauses built into the Memorandum and Articles of Association of the company which automatically transferred shares between directors upon the death of any one of us. I now owned 54% of the company, Mark Hopkins owned 41% and Art owned just 5%. I had complete control. I had enough shares to make any decisions I wanted and I could not be outvoted. Basically the Black Moon company was mine. Even if Art sold out to Mark – which was highly improbable – I would still have more than half the shares – which meant 100% control.

There was a downside to the way events had unfolded - potentially dangerous events. Julio and his cronies would not be held for long. The henchmen would get out almost immediately – after all they had only been driving in a car behind the suspect. Julio would have a little more trouble getting released but would no doubt have the legal backup from his friends in Italy to get out on bail within days. He would be angry and looking for revenge. It would not take him long to come to the conclusion that he had been set up as the fall guy by the people behind the killing. Somebody would come after me – that was certain.

I visited Paul Nixon in Bristol and he arranged for a couple of goons to accompany me for a few weeks until they had made their move or decided that they had lost very little apart from some pride. Nobody is indispensable in the world of organised crime and the Italians had gained total control of my car racket. They would no longer have to fit Johnny Walsh into their plans or share the lucrative profits with him. Julio would be free again – the murder weapon did not have his fingerprints on it. It could have been planted in his car while he was inside Johnny Walsh's house. Such things had been done before!!

As it turned out I got a letter from Julio a couple of weeks later, thanking me for gifting him a lucrative car business. I took that to mean he had forgiven me my little joke and felt he had gained more than he had lost. He was probably as happy as I was about the death of Johnny Walsh. I sent the two security assistants back to Paul with my thanks.

I didn't feel bad about the loss of the stolen car operation. It had started to get rather complicated and even though the profits had been good, they were nothing compared to those we received from the legitimate car parts business which Art Mercer had expanded very impressively. We now had over 50 employees – all paying the correct amount of tax, all completely above board.

I was beginning to consider going completely straight regarding my retail projects. I was getting rich and felt less like risking it all if I didn't have to. I was confident that Art and Mark would be likely to feel the same – Art had told me as much and Mark was enjoying his wealth too much to be bothered with the intricacies of running a criminal enterprise. The fact was – I was no longer getting enough of a buzz from these activities. I was ready to move on to an even more audacious, daring and potentially lucrative business idea which had been brewing in my twisted mind for some time.

G10 Security had proved itself. With the disposal of Johnny Walsh, the company had moved into a whole new area of operation. I had been thinking for some time about ways to make more money – gain more power whilst taking less risk and making less effort. Stealing cars and shipping them to Italy had seemed a good idea at the time but it involved a lot of people – a lot of potential weak links in the chain. The costs of running such an organisation had been high. I had come up with a much better option – and G10 would be at the very heart of it.

I wanted to make more gains for less effort – so it was an obvious next step to employ less people. With the Mafia now controlling the car racket, it made no sense to keep it going my end – so it was shut down during the next month – certain employees were given large 'golden parachutes' – a sort of retirement pension paid as a lump sum as a thank you for all their hard work.

The cigarette and booze side of the business was also terminated in like fashion. Dermot Leach received a fat payout and was happy with it. He had enough wealth to prefer comfort over risk. I made sure that everyone was happy and feeling that they had been treated fairly – or more than fairly. I didn't want bitter people sticking the knife in at some later stage.

The only two enterprises still ongoing were the legitimate Black Moon company – dealing in auto parts – and more recently marine engines – Art couldn't fully give up on his old ways – and the G10 company – also legit on paper, though actually the master key to my new enterprise.

Paul Nixon was in charge of the day to day running of the business, he had contacts everywhere – some of them incredibly shady and secretive. I was more of a guiding light for the company – setting the goals and targets for expansion of the enterprise.

Our primary services – the legal ones – were the regular supply of security agents and event management to the rich and famous – everything from bouncers to entire security teams for pop concerts, business seminars and other large gatherings.

The dark side of the business was likely to prove considerably more lucrative – but would need to be kept secret from the regular employees of the company.

Only Paul, myself and the agents or operatives carrying out the tasks would need to know anything of the criminal side of the organisation. Paul was sure he had the right people for the job. His arrangement of Johnny Walsh's demise seemed to prove that to be true.

As well as acting as an assassination bureau, the company would engage in the blackmail of some of the same celebrities and business people we were paid to protect – it was simple. We become indispensable protectors of people with secrets – they pay us for this, obviously. Then we use the secrets we have discovered to blackmail them for huge sums of cash. Finally we are paid other large amounts of cash to find out who is behind the blackmail and stop them - possibly by assassinating them – drawing even larger fees – and also getting proof that they paid to have people killed – giving us ultimate control over them.

It was not beyond the bounds of belief that we could quickly gain full control over certain sectors of government, the military and business, by employing such methods.

I couldn't help smiling when I thought about how many of these ideas had been placed in my mind by the vivid coma dreams I had endured after my serious injury in that terrorist attack a few years ago. The injuries had created in me the need for excitement and danger which motivated me to get involved in these lucrative activities – the old me would never have thought it worth the effort – the old me was a nobody – going nowhere slowly. I had been changed by fate – and I was enjoying every minute of it. My moral compass may have slipped considerably but I saw that as a plus, rather than a minus.

Art was happy running Black Moon Ltd – and Paul Nixon was happy running G10 Security Ltd. I owned the majority shareholding in both companies – had full control and the largest share of the profits – it was a nice situation to be in.

Mark Hopkins was not involved in the G10 operation – in fact I had not told him or Art anything about it. He continued to indulge his growing desire for luxury living – buying a large country house and a big yacht, currently moored in Cannes. As long as he got his fair share of the fat profits he was more than happy to let me get on with it.

I took a short sailing holiday once things had been set up to my liking – *Black Moon* was a pleasure to sail – her smooth, powerful movement through the water added a sense of quality to the experience.

I crossed the English Channel and soon passed Dungeness, turning into the North Sea. I was in no hurry, had no firm destination. I just wanted a bit of space. I needed to take time out to relax and rest. Things were going well for me. I was rich, successful and happy. I had plans for the businesses – both illegal and straight. I could see things becoming even more lucrative and stimulating. My need for danger and excitement was satisfied by my current activities.

My only slight concern was that I was entering into some very dark areas of operation – I had already been responsible for the killing of one man – my old friend Johnny Walsh. This caused me some uncomfortable feelings and some sleepless nights. It was hard to come to terms with.

I began to wonder if some of my newly acquired personality traits and behaviours were driven by a subconscious effect of the coma. I saw similarities between my coma dreams and the things I was now doing, which unsettled me. I had not only had Johnny Walsh's head blown off and planted the shotgun in someone else's vehicle – but I was now running a secret criminal organisation which I had named G10. The irony was not lost on me.

The old, pre-accident me would never have caused anyone's death. The old me would not be thinking of blackmailing people or needing to gain power and control over areas of government – it sounded crazy to the old me – a bit of whom still remained below the surface of my psyche.

On the other hand, the old me was lazy, bored and pointless. He had achieved nothing, stood for nothing and had nothing. Good Riddance to him!

Johnny Walsh had got what he deserved – he was a sneaky cheating disloyal bastard and I was glad to see the back of him. The fact that I had arranged for his demise to echo the coma dreams was just a case of my twisted sense of humour kicking in. My naming of the security company G10, was likewise a bit of fun which made me chuckle. No more than that. If the activities of *my* G10 and the *fictional* G10 happened to show similarities, then so be it. Ideas had to come from somewhere so why not from my unconscious mind.

I pulled myself together and celebrated with a double thickness ham sandwich. I wolfed it down as usual and nearly choked – but a few swigs of Morgan's straight from the bottle soon sorted that out. I was fired up again – ready to step up to the next level. I had plans which would make my previous escapades seem paltry by comparison.

I decided I had had enough holiday for now – holiday from what? I asked myself. Holiday from doing the things I love doing, which give me a sense of satisfaction and bring me wealth, power and control? Who the fuck needs a holiday from that? Not me, that's for sure.

I turned my boat around and headed back to my kingdom.

Chapter 24

I was energised, excited, ready for action. I spent a few days talking to all my chess pieces – mainly pawns but also a couple of Knights and Rooks. Then I went to see the Bishop - Paul Nixon. I spoke with him intensely over a few days and not only assured myself that I could trust him, but that he had the plans and manpower required to carry out our first major foray into the world of blackmail. I was the Queen – the most powerful - and the King – the most important - on my chessboard. I was the scriptwriter, the director, the Star.

Our first victim was a local politician – he was a big cheese in the Hampshire County Council – and just a little practise run for G10. We didn't really need him. We wanted to test out our new enterprise on somebody of little real importance, but with enough power to be of some use. We wanted him in our pocket, as the saying goes.

All it took was a pretty girl who bewitched him at a civic function, some hidden cameras and bingo! He was ours. The old Badger game never fails!

An agent of G10 approached him discretely one evening, showed him the photos and gave him a password to remember. He was to obey any instructions he received which included the password – it was as simple as that. He knew the photos would ruin his career – and his marriage – if he dared challenge our authority. He never did.

We let him off lightly, not really needing him for anything more than planning permissions to be rushed through for some local builders who were paying us to short cut the system for them. It went smoothly. No hitches.

Our second try-out was a sergeant in the stores of an army base situated in a bleak part of Scotland – which includes most of it – the sort of army base nobody ever visits and where the soldiers are badly trained and ill-disciplined. We used the same girl and the same cameras. It was like falling off a log. He was able to supply us with a few machine guns and a mortar. The paperwork was so sloppy in the stores that it was unlikely the disappearance of a few weapons would be noticed – at least not for a considerable time. I was pleased with how this particular project had gone – he might come in handy in the future.

Over the next nine months we extended our operations into several fields of endeavour. Politicians were the easiest due to their natural greed and lack of morals. We built up a nice little collection of them, based in all parts of the UK, including our first Cabinet Minister.

We also managed to acquire a selection of police officers, mainly middle rank, but a couple of nice juicy Superintendents too. They would come in very handy some day.

We trapped a few journalists – some quite big names working in TV and major newspapers. Our first Editor followed soon after – we now had control over the front page of a Red Top daily newspaper. Things were proceeding nicely.

Over time I developed an expanded strategy which further strengthened our grip over those we had blackmailed into doing our bidding. I decided it would be a good idea to add a juicy carrot to supplement the stick.

Any of our victims – or partners as we started referring to them – who satisfactorily obeyed the instructions we gave them three times – were put on our payroll. Each time they carried out our orders successfully, we would reward them with cash payments. For example, one chief superintendent of police who had used his influence to cancel a drunk driving charge against our people for a third time, received an envelope full of cash through his letterbox - £5,000 to be precise. From then on he was only too keen to offer his services willingly. He jumped fully on board. It changed his view of his predicament to one of great promise. He even suggested ways in which he could help us, which we hadn't asked him to. He knew a few magistrates who might be useful and even gave us some 'dirt' on them so we could get our claws into them. We had them under our wing quickly, paid the Superintendent a 'finders fee' of £3,000 per magistrate. It's amazing how quickly corruption can spread.

One area we wanted to gain influence in, which was not quite so easy, was the British Secret Service. Not because their agents are less corruptible but because they are less identifiable – after all they are part of a 'secret' organisation. We did begin to make some progress in this area however.

We had 'recruited' a police officer who worked for Special Branch – the police department which carries out operations on behalf of MI5 and MI6 –

he was able to give us information regarding covert operatives – 'secret agents'.

It didn't take long to get a number of agents working for us. We not only gathered large quantities of 'evidence' against them but we paid a lot better than the British government.

Within six months we had about 10% of the British Secret Service on our payroll. We knew most of what the government knew and inspired a lot more loyalty from our operatives.

From the information gained via these British Agents, we were able to extend our sneaky fingers into the American Secret Service, military and government. If anything they were even more corrupt than our own MPs. Most were on the 'fiddle' before we got to them and we moved through their ranks like wildfire.

We got a senior adviser to the president in our pocket, along with a couple of US generals, top brass at the pentagon, important people in the CIA and FBI and many more. We were becoming a global force – a sort of worldwide army of criminality – sucking up all the power, using it for our own purposes. I was now what could be termed a 'Supervillain' as seen in Bond movies.

I even had a secret lair built. I used my influence on several high ranking Intelligence Service officials to gain ownership of an abandoned underground facility beneath the streets of Whitehall, had my own top people brought in to secure it from unwanted pests – the legitimate Secret Service people for example. This became my main Command Centre – from where I ran operations and directed my agents.

I received complete loyalty from my people –
we paid them exceedingly well – far more than they
could hope to gain by being loyal to the 'powers
that be' – or the 'powers that used to be' as I
referred to them. Not only that but we made a point
of increasing the amount of evidence against them.
Each time somebody undertook criminal activities
on our behalf – we gathered evidence of them
doing it. They now had even more to lose if they
ever thought of betraying us. They also knew we
wasted no time in eliminating anyone who stood in
our way.

It was mind blowing. I sometimes had to take
a couple of days off – sailing my boat, getting some
fresh air - attempting to get everything into
perspective. It was like some cheap paperback
novel – but it was actually happening.

I spent a fair amount of time in meetings with
Paul Nixon who was proving himself reliable and
efficient. The man was a machine. If he said he
would do something, it got done. I relied upon him
to an increased degree. To be honest he was the
real driving force behind our success. I was in
overall charge and had the final say on what the
G10 organisation did and didn't do – but it was Paul
who saw that my orders were carried out quickly
and fully. We were a good team. Which is why it
was such a devastating blow when I was awoken
one morning by a phone call informing me that Paul
Nixon had been assassinated. It was the initial
move by certain forces which had declared war on
G10 – and on me personally.

Chapter 25

I had no idea who was behind the killing of Paul Nixon. The list of potential suspects was as long and slippery as an octopus tentacle. With my most trusted advisor gone, I had nobody I could rely on to get me out of the situation. We had so many powerful, resentful people on our payroll that I would not know where to begin looking. I had no idea what to do about it. I was lost. Paul had been the rock on which the organisation rested – the strategist who planned our moves. Now G10 was a headless chicken racing around all over the place.

I contacted some key people – Paul's second in command was a man named Felix Hudson – a man I knew little and trusted not at all because I knew him so little. I spoke to some of the powerful people under G10 control – though for how much longer they might remain so was a question I could not answer – and was told by all of them that they knew nothing. They would have said that in any case – sensing a chance to get free of the G10 stranglehold, seeing opportunities for revenge on the horizon. I couldn't blame them. It was only fair after what we had put them through, how we had exploited them and threatened them.

It was clear that word was out, that we were floundering in chaos – the wolves were gathering, teeth bared, ready to rip G10 – and their once so cocky leader – to pieces.

I had no intention of letting that happen. I didn't hang around in a desperate attempt to somehow stave off the inevitable for a few months. I could read the writing on the wall. I had to get out – abandon everything. I had done it before and I now had to do it again. Things could not be saved – that was the sort of foolish thinking which could get me killed. It was time to skedaddle. Shit or bust. Maybe just Bust this time.

The strange thing was, I didn't care that my evil empire was crumbling before my eyes – I had started to find it a bore. It would be a relief to have a new start – go back to the simple happy times of my ignorant past. That's what I told myself anyway as I climbed aboard *Black Moon,* piloted her out into the English Channel once more – this time would be the last.

I didn't have to think where I wanted to go – I was sick of the North Sea, so I went South – heading for warmer climes. It took me a week to reach the French coastal town of Biarritz – close to the Spanish border. I moored up here – among the millionaires yachts, spent a week sunning myself and drinking too much. Whatever was going to happen to me – whether I was to be the victim of a very expensive hit-man or arrested and thrown in jail for the rest of my life – it would not happen before I had as much time as possible enjoying myself. I was on a permanent holiday, had enough cash and gold coins with me to last until I expired from over-indulgence.

The casino in Biarritz was on my side too it seemed – I was not usually one for gambling but I felt it would be fun to risk a couple of thousand on the Roulette tables as I was in a gamblers paradise

– and blow me if I didn't come out of the place 20 grand up. I guess when your luck is in it's in.

I was enjoying the slow, lazy pace of life – it fitted in with my natural lazy streak. I got back underway after seven days and moved west – along the southern edge of the Bay of Biscay – the Spanish coast on my port side just within view.

The seas were gentle – it was summer after all – and the warmth of the sun gave me a sense of security and health. I had built up the stores in my boat before I left England. There was plenty of food, drink, fresh water for me and the engine – as well as diesel (for the engine).

I spent the next few days stuffing my face and toasting the future – I was feeling more optimistic with each day that passed. My transponder had been switched off – which was illegal but meant that my craft could not be tracked via satellite. The chances of anyone happening to spot my boat as it smoothly sailed the warm blue waters of Biscay and turned south around the Portuguese headland were slim in the extreme.

I knew that whoever had been behind the murder of Paul Nixon would have a lot of spies in ports worldwide – I would be taking a risk every time I moored up – but out at sea it was a million to one chance they would find me, though I was somewhat concerned that one of my enemy's agents may spot the name on the side of my boat.

I dropped anchor twenty miles off the coast of Portugal and launched my dinghy. It took me under an hour to paint out the name on the keel – both sides – with some black paint I had on board. It looked great. Unless some spy had a very good description of my boat and recognised it as a

Westsail 32 painted black, they would be unlikely to report it. There were a lot of different boats in and out of every harbour in the world – a lot of them had black keels – a lot of them looked vaguely similar to my boat. If all the spies reported every black boat of approximately the same size as mine – it would take my enemies a very long time to investigate all of them. They would probably have no more than a handful of assassins primed to take me out – and by the time they had been notified of my possible location I would no longer be there. It might set them on my trail but there was a lot of ocean out there and a few incorrect sightings added to the correct one of my boat would very quickly complicate matters. I felt I had a very good chance of eluding them – particularly as I was fast becoming unrecognisable, my skin becoming darker each day and my hair lightening as the sun bleached the colour out of it. A good pair of shades, some hair lengthening, and I looked just like every other boat gypsy haunting the ports of the world.

It was possible that there were no killers looking for me at all – the people behind recent events had smashed my organisation, gained control of it. Unless they were particularly out for revenge – which was likely but not certain – it was possible that they would be happy with their victory over G10 and leave it at that. If I happened to appear on their radar they would no doubt send someone to 'look after me' but it was probable they would not spend too long actively scouring the planet for a glimpse of me.

If I played it cool I should be fairly safe. I refuelled in a little harbour, spent a few hours sunning myself on the nearby Praia de São

Bernadino. The beach was hot, full of tourists and noisy – I enjoyed the anonymity it offered. It was good to be among normal people doing nothing more than enjoying life.

I kept travelling South for further week, until I reached the waters of North Africa. Here it was very hot close to land but the sea breezes made it more bearable. I stayed out to sea – well off the coast during the day – only venturing landward as the evening cooled things down a little. I would anchor off the coast and enjoy watching the lights of the coastal towns.

I had been at sea for a while now and decided to moor at Tangier in Morocco – that mighty and ancient maritime city founded by the Phoenicians 1000 years BC. The population was close to 1 million people. I made it close to one million and one.

I spent a few days visiting the markets and bars of the city. I stocked up on a few provisions, undertook some minor maintenance on my boat, including having the name 'Freedom' painted on the keel to replace the old name Black Moon. I had toyed with the idea of having the entire keel painted a different colour but decided against it.

I planned to move back out to sea the next morning and was just battening down the hatches for the night when I noticed a man watching me. I had seen him before – hanging around my boat, observing my movements but it was only now that it dawned on me he might be a spy. If I went back to sea now he would be able to report this to whoever he may be working for and they would find me easily – somewhere far from land – I would be easy pickings in such isolated waters. A helicopter or a fast powerboat would easily outpace me wherever I went. So I went nowhere. I kept an eye on him, even as he kept an eye on me. I had an advantage in this because I knew he was observing me but not vice versa – he had no idea that I had spotted him. I decided next morning to turn this to my advantage.

I got up, had breakfast on board and peeped over the deck to make sure he was still there. He was. I locked up, went down the jetty – walking slowly into town in a nonchalant manner. He kept quite a distance from me but never lost touch completely – he obviously knew what he was doing – a professional. I let him get confident that I was unaware of his presence. Then around noon I walked around a corner and hid behind a large tree which grew at the side of the street.

My tracker came round the corner and walked past me. He seemed unconcerned that I was no longer in sight – the street was a short one and no doubt he thought I would be just around the next corner. When he found that I wasn't he stayed calm – he could always go back to the harbour and wait for me to return to my boat.

He shrugged and turned back – heading the way we had come. This time it was me who did the following. I knew he would go back to the boat eventually but given that he thought I was off in town shopping and sightseeing, it was unlikely that he would go there straight away. I wanted to see where he would go – if he would contact anyone else.

He spent half an hour in a cafe, drinking mint tea and chatting to a couple sitting nearby – tourists. Then he paid his bill, started off into the centre of a large market area – it was fairly crowded and I could follow him with little likelihood of him spotting me – after all he didn't expect me to be there so would not be overcautious.

Once inside the souk, the indoor market, I walked casually, pretending to look at some of the goods which were on display. The Moroccan traders were quick to spot a potential buyer and I had to be assertive in my determination not to be sidetracked and lose my quarry. He for his part was starting to look like a man on a mission – he marched straight, giving no eye contact to the sellers. His pace picked up and I once had to run to get back on his trail when he disappeared from my sight.

Eventually we reached a quieter area. I saw him sit down at a table outside a small busy cafe. A man came out of the place and he said something in Arabic. The man went back inside, came out with another man, who sat at the spy's table. Julio Montefiore. Obviously a man willing to hold a grudge.

I turned on my heel, got out of the souk as quickly as I could – which wasn't very quick – it was a labyrinth of twists, turns and criss-crossing paths. Eventually I did find my way back to the harbour and wasted no time in getting my boat out to sea. I had considered selling the boat to a local for peanuts on condition that they go far out to sea and avoid all other craft for a few days – to lead my pursuers on a merry dance while I made other arrangements for my escape. In the end I just couldn't bring myself to abandon *Black Moon* – I was attached to her and would have to risk paying a price for my loyalty.

I was out of sight of land within an hour. I was confident that my spy would not return to the harbour for at least a couple of hours. I had a small head start – and with the transponder turned off I would not be trackable by electronic means. I had no idea how many boats, planes and helicopters Montefiori could call up to scour the seas but I was willing to risk it.

By nightfall I was twenty miles off the coast and heading out into the North Atlantic on a South-Westerly course. My boat was not fast so I had to rely on luck to protect me from my foes. Darkness was my friend. I could relax at night – I turned off all my running lights and my boat became virtually invisible. I was fairly close to the equator now so the split between day and night was almost fifty fifty – I could expect around 12 hours of darkness. This would allow me to travel at least 200 miles overnight – possibly 300 if there was enough wind to push me along faster than my engine could manage.

I was in luck – a strong breeze did in fact build up overnight – nothing dangerous – just powerful enough and in the right direction for me to cruise through the ocean at almost 30 knots.

Even if Montefiori had jets out searching for me he would not be able to see much at night and the range of smaller jets was not so great as to allow him to sweep whole swathes of ocean in all directions looking for me. I could move in a single straight line – he would have to cross and recross vast fields of water – because he would not know where I was heading – dammit I didn't even know where I was heading!

149

Helicopters had short range – and boats would be much slower – they may be faster than *Black Moon* but they would also have to sweep the seas – rather than just coming at me in a straight line. They would also not be able to search at night whereas I could still move away quickly. I began to feel elated, that their chances of catching me were low in the extreme.

The only way they might find me is when I landed to take on supplies – after all that was how they had found me in Morocco. I decided I would be better off docking in smaller coastal harbours, keeping away from popular, busy cities.

As I approached the Equator I turned onto a Westerly course, headed towards the West Indies. I had been to Barbados on holiday a few years ago, had found the locals to be friendly and not too keen to help the authorities. I had stayed in contact – albeit rarely and not for a few years – with a local fisherman named Ricky Robinson. I had no idea if he was still around but thought it likely he was – his family had been involved in the fishing game for two generations and he also made money by taking tourists out on fishing trips.

My water and fuel were starting to run out – not desperate yet but low enough to make me keen to get into a port and restock.

I used the sails as much as possible, conserved my drinking water as best I could. I reckoned I could make it to Barbados without stopping anywhere else along the way – not that there are many places you can pull into in the middle of the Atlantic ocean.

After two days – still no sign of my pursuers – I was getting thirsty – my water supplies had not gone as far as I had estimated. There were other liquids aboard – tinned soups, fruit juice and ice cubes in the freezer. These added another couple of days to how long I could last.

Unfortunately the weather was getting much hotter as I moved into the Caribbean Sea. I slept as much as possible to conserve water – it helped a bit although I still felt thirsty while I was asleep and had some strange dreams about deserts with fountains shooting up out of the sand. I also lost my appetite as I consumed less water – the heat made me angry but I had to keep calm if possible.

I was losing weight – which initially I viewed as a good thing but my face started looking like a skeleton and I didn't like it any more after seeing that. I would just have to put up with it for now and hope that the winds would be kind to me.

They weren't. I had to start up my engines and this increased the heat and noise on board to a considerable degree. I couldn't decide whether to commit suicide or smash the boat up in anger – these were the extremes of emotion I was experiencing. I was at the end of my tether. It was only when I heard the sound of a helicopter somewhere out on the horizon, that I pulled myself together. It may have been an innocent businessman travelling to some sales seminar, or regular cargo traffic delivering to one of the smaller islands which were beginning to appear in the distance. I knew it was neither of these things. My skin crawled, my mind freaked, I began to sweat even more than I already was. I knew without a shadow of a doubt that someone had found me. Someone knew precisely where I was and they were coming directly towards my little boat.

I went below, grabbed a Kalashnikov machine gun. I had a good supply of weapons on board. If the 'copter came within range I would blast it out of the sky, whoever was on board. My main concern was that it would not come within range – it didn't need to – all they had to do was track me until I moored up – then they could send their agents to get me at their leisure.

I was days away from Barbados and would be a sitting duck if I pulled into any of the small unnamed islands which were getting a little nearer now. I was in a trap whatever I did. I could see no way out of the situation – not any way that I liked.

I eventually reasoned that if I could get onto one of the little islands I might be in a position to at least have a fighting chance. Once I docked in a large country harbour I would have nowhere left to run – they would have men waiting for me before I even arrived. My only hope was to get rid of the helicopter and its crew before they knew where I was precisely heading. I would rather fight a few men in a helicopter than a whole army in a large town.

I could see a small island over to my starboard side – roughly ten miles away by my reckoning – which depended on my guess as to the size of the island – was it small or very far away? There was no way I could be sure but I had no other option so I headed straight for it. Obviously the helicopter would get there before me and they would be waiting to finish me off as I washed up on the shore. My only hope was that I could think of some way of getting them before they got me. Whatever happened it was my best chance – they could have no more than five or six men aboard their craft and they would almost certainly not expect me to have a lot of very potent weapons on my boat – or have the nerve to come out fighting. I felt I had a chance.

I was weakened due to lack of water but no so bad I couldn't become active if I needed to – and I would definitely need to. I could now see that the island was mainly rocky – at least the side of it I could see from where I was. The helicopter had begun to move towards the island – they had obviously seen my course change, probably thought I was trying to hide on the island.

Ten minutes later the helicopter moved across the island and disappeared from my view as it descended behind a high rock. From the sound of its engines I could tell that they had landed – there would be a welcoming committee. I moved into position, let the boat move slowly in towards a sandy cove I had spotted as I got nearer. I was now less than half a mile from the island.

I could not see anyone on the shore – they had probably decided to lie in wait – until I beached my boat. I would then be a sitting duck.

The boat moved forward, edging onto the low sandy beach, eventually running aground on the sand bar which fronted the island edge. Immediately four men moved down towards the boat, two of them carrying handguns, another held a machine gun. The man at the back was keeping his distance – he was obviously the boss – he wore a fancy suit which looked out of place in this environment – maybe it was Julio himself – I couldn't see him clearly from my position.

As they began to swarm onto my boat, I climbed out of the water – fifty yards to the left of my boat. I had gone into the water half a mile out and made my way to a slightly raised area which gave me a good view of what was happening on the beach. The Kalashnikov felt good in my hands – it had been submerged, slung over my shoulder as I swam toward the rocks – but would not be affected in the short term by the water.

I crept out into view and fired at the men as they came off my boat – shaking their heads at the lack of one Michael Garvie onboard. The man with the machine gun was my first target – he was the most dangerous,. He went down under a hail of bullets, dropping his gun and screaming in pain. The remaining three men turned and twisted their heads – attempting to figure out where the shots had come from. One of them saw me and dived behind a rock but the other gunman was too slow and I blasted him into oblivion. Now it was two against one.

The guy in the suit – I could now see that it was indeed Julio Montefiore – had taken a pistol from inside his jacket and ducked down behind a scrubby plant which spread out almost ten yards wide. He would be able to move behind this small thicket and adapt his angle of fire as I moved in.

The man behind the rock was only a few feet away from the machine gun which his dead companion had discarded when he fell. I really didn't want him to get hold of it as I was not experienced in this kind of shoot out whereas I could be fairly certain that he would be – I would be more prone to strategic errors than he would – plus there were two of them and only one of me. I kept my eyes firmly planted on the discarded weapon – as long as it was still there I was reasonably safe.

A movement to my left caused me to flick my focus to Julio – who I saw running low from the end of the hedge and across a short expanse of sand – gaining the shelter of a large rocky outcrop which would give him the opportunity to make his way round behind me. When I looked back at the machine gun it was gone. I was in trouble.

I moved back a little, climbed behind a big outcrop which I thought would probably continue around to where I had seen Julio move. He could appear around a corner at any moment. The guy with the machine gun was also out of my line of sight too. I didn't know where they were. They however knew where I was. It was a classic pincer movement – with them closing in from both sides.

I had one hope. If either of the gunmen came into view before the other I would have a chance to shoot him before the other could shoot me from the back. If they synchronised their attack to appear from opposite directions simultaneously I was finished. It was shit or bust.

I waited for my fate to be revealed – felt my legs shaking with fear as I did so. Sweat dripped into my eyes. I did not want to die.

I heard a sound to my left – I swivelled, raising my gun as I turned. There was the guy with the machine gun – we saw each other at the exact same time – racing to fire our weapon before our opponent could. I heard a sound to my right – dived to the ground. Gunfire – a pistol and a barrage of bullets from the machine gun. It surprised me that I heard the bullets – I had always thought you could not hear the bullet which killed you.

I heard screaming. I had not been killed. The shooting stopped. I looked up. There was a dead man nearby. It was Julio Montefiore – shot to pieces, riddled with machine gun rounds. I turned my head – waiting for the assassin to finish me off. He was close by. I trembled as I looked over towards him. I was surprised to see that he was also dead - from a single pistol shot to the head. I had survived by a miracle – they had shot each other – I had dived at the exact moment they fired – and they had killed each other instead of me. If they had not appeared at the same time at least one of them might be alive and I would almost certainly be one of the corpses littering these rocks.

I stood up – still shaking – the adrenaline had not drained away yet. I stumbled towards the body of the assassin – his Kalashnikov was on the ground next to him. I dragged it away from him – you can't be too careful – and went through his pockets. I found his wallet. It contained no identification – just a few currency notes – 200 American Dollars. I took them and stashed them in my jacket pocket. Julio was carrying a bigger stash – he had his passport and driver's licence on him too – not that he would be needing either of them ever again. I took the 3,000 Euros and stored them with the dollars. It would go some way towards paying for the fear and inconvenience they had caused me.

I left the bodies uncovered – the ground was too rocky to dig graves and I didn't really want to drag them all the way across the beach for a sea burial. I crouched low as I made my way over a small hill, attempting to find the helicopter they had arrived in. I had to be careful – there may be a pilot to contend with – or other killers who had stayed out of sight.

I saw the 'copter sitting in the middle of a small expanse of bare earth. There were low bushes around part of this area. I nipped behind some shrubbery, glanced across to where the aircraft sat – engines off and appearing empty. It was quite possible that one of the people I had killed had been the pilot. On the other hand there could be men lying in wait – maybe they had heard the shooting and taken cover.

I made my way around in a clockwise direction – getting closer to the craft. Still no sign of life. I waited, watching and alert, for quarter of an hour but nothing happened so I crawled out from behind the bush, ran in a crouched position towards the helicopter. I got in close to the fuselage and moved slowly toward the side door.

"OK Big Boy – just you freeze right there" said a voice from behind me. The voice did not sound at all confident – in fact the person speaking sounded scared stiff.

"Ok, just stay calm fella – I'm not moving a muscle". I was concerned that if this person who sounded so nervous had a gun on me – and it was very likely that he did – that any kind of sudden – or not so sudden move on my part could cause him to freak out and shoot me on the spot. My mind was thinking in quick time – being in a deadly situation can have that effect – I reasoned that he must be the pilot – it made sense that he had waited in or near to the helicopter – and it also added up that he was not really experienced in gunfights – he flew things – that was his job and that was where his experience lay.

"Move away from the chopper" it was more of a suggestion than a command. I put my hands in the air to signify my compliance – even though he had not told me to do so – and moved backwards. As I did so I very slowly turned to face my opponent.

"You must be the pilot?" I enquired. He nodded rather timidly. I'm not looking to cause you any trouble" I spoke in a calm, friendly manner. "It was your pals who came here to kill me, remember – I just got them before they got me. I have no fight with you".

"Well, that's nice to know" he said. "All I wanna do is get away safely and go back to normal life – that sound fair to you Mr?"

"That's what I want too mate. No need for us to be falling out is there?"

"So how we gonna play it then?" he asked.

"I've got a boat – you've got this chopper – why don't we just agree to go our separate ways?"

"That's pretty much the idea I had too Mister – just don't go shooting me down with that there Kalashnikov"

"Take it with you – then I'm unarmed".

"That sounds right to me".

"I could do with a couple of little favours if you think you can maybe help me – you see I'm very short of water and a bit low on diesel fuel too. If you've any spare water I could have – just a few litres would be fantastic – I would then be able to make it to civilisation in one piece".

"That shouldn't be a problem – I can let you have five litres – we carry plenty on board. Can't help you with the diesel though".

"I don't actually need diesel with the wind in the right direction – that's not the other favour"

"Well what is then?"

"I need you to not report to your bosses until I can get to safety – there are a lot of very powerful and highly dangerous people out looking for me and I would appreciate a reasonable head start".

"I can do that – there's no way I'm going back alone to a bunch of killers and telling them all the other killers were killed and that you escaped – and I somehow survived – they would instantly be suspicious of that – I don't even know them – I just got hired to fly this heap out here on a 'rescue mission' – that's what they told me – didn't know there was going to be a load of killing. This is way out of my league – I'm skedaddling right back to Santa Monica – where I know people – family – I've only been out here in the West Indies for a couple of months – now I'm caught up in bad shit – not my cup of tea pal – I'm not going to say anything to no-one" He was rambling – no doubt from a mixture of relief and adrenaline.

"Hey pal, take a breath". I moved back so he could pick up the fallen machine gun. He placed it inside the cockpit of the helicopter and brought me a five litre bottle of water.

"There you go fella – hope you make it to somewhere safe".

"Likewise to you man" I replied. We both shrugged to each other in a comradely manner. Then he got back in the copter, started the engines – the wind from the rotors blew sand all over me, so I dived to the ground. He lifted off. I stood up and watched the craft move higher. I waved to the pilot. He waved back and quickly the aircraft became smaller until it disappeared over the horizon.

I took a deep breath and made my way back to *Black Moon*. She had not been damaged – I was relieved. I took a long swig of water – it tasted like ambrosia mixed with nectar. I had to use all the willpower I could muster to not drink it all in one go – I would need it later if I was to survive.

It was getting dark as I cast off and returned to the relative safety of the ocean. The winds were fairly strong but luckily they were in the right direction. I moved through the water with relief. I was not out of danger – but it felt like I was, so I tried to enjoy it.

Chapter 26

Three days later I reached Barbados. I used some fake identity papers in the name of Chris Denby which the customs guys had no interest in at all – it was hot and they were in island mode. If the temperature went above 25 degrees centigrade it was generally accepted that it was too hot to exert yourself – so most people slowed down, relaxed and became substantially more inert. It seemed a good idea to me and suited my purposes. I didn't want anyone knowing I was here - and according to my papers and the name on my boat – I wasn't here.

I moored, walked into the nearest little town – where I hired a motorcycle – a battered old Honda CB 250 – and started out towards the home – or the last known address to be more accurate – of my acquaintance Ricky Robinson.

As I approached his house I could see him sitting on the porch – a straw hat pulled down over his eyes. He looked up as he heard the sound of a motorbike. I pulled up beside his verandah and he gave me an odd look – obviously didn't recognise me – maybe he couldn't even remember me – it had been a while.

"Hey Ricky – how's tricks?" I shouted. He stared, studying my face. Failed to know me.

"Who are you man and whadya want?" I got off the bike and came closer – I was not wearing a crash helmet – it was optional in these parts. He still didn't seem to recognise me.

"Mike Garvie – it's been a while – I may have changed a bit since you last saw me". At the name Mike Garvie – he sat up straight – looked a bit startled even.

"You better come into the house man". He stood and led the way into the small front room of his cosy but cramped home. It looked just like I remembered it all those years ago when I had first met him. He relaxed his face once we were indoors.

"How's things Ricky" I asked "Still taking the tourists for trips around the island?"

"Mainly fishin' these days – but never mind that – there's been a couple of heavy dudes out here asking about you – they are payin' good money for information about you man – what kinda trouble you in?"

I gave him a description of the two henchmen I had dispatched on the remote island a few days ago – he recognised their description. "That sounds like 'em – what did you do to get them so keen to find you?"

I laughed "You wouldn't believe me if I told you"

"Try me – I'll believe just about anything once I get me some Captain's inside me" He pulled out a bottle of Morgan's Spiced rum – it was he who had got me started on it in the first place – and poured two generous glasses of the amber liquid.

"Sorry I ain't got no ice – I had some but it melted".

"No problem – thanks" I took a large sip and put my glass down on the sideboard. "You better have a few more of these Ricky, before I tell you what I've been up to – cos even you are gonna have trouble getting your head around it".

"You let me be the judge of that". He poured himself a refill, passed the bottle to me so I could do the same.

Two hours later his eyes were out on stalks.

"Holy Moly man – if even half of what you just told me is true I'm surprised you're still walking and talking".

"You're not the only one" I replied.

I spent the night at Ricky's place – drinking rum, eating mango and chilli con carne. I slept like a baby – a drunken baby.

The next day I went to the local town market with Ricky and bought some supplies – food and bottled water. We went into a dark, cool cafe and I drank three cups of horrendous tea while Ricky spoke to some of his contacts.

It transpired that most of them had been approached by Montefiore or his henchmen – who had been willing to pay for information regarding my whereabouts. Fortunately none of the locals knew me, so their enquiries had fallen on stony ground. In the end I had simply been spotted from the helicopter. Now that problem was solved - assuming that it had been a private vendetta pursued by Julio in revenge for the trouble I had caused him in the past. If that *was* the case, it meant that someone else may have been behind the sudden and dramatic takeover of G10 and the assassination of Paul Nixon.

The fact that Julio himself had come for me tended to indicate that it was personal. I doubted he had enough importance to set such powerful wheels in motion as would have been necessary to gain control of my whole operation in one fell swoop. I could not explain how Julio had tracked me down at all – there were millions of square miles of ocean out there and he had found out I was somewhere near Barbados. He must have been acting on information received.

It brought to mind some of the experiences I'd had whilst in my coma. The powerful secret forces working against me and me not knowing how they could possibly have found me. It was weird. I sensed an evil presence behind the destruction of my global enterprise. In my dreams it had been Johnny Walsh – but in reality he was now dead. Or was he? Had I personally seen him shot? No I had not. The thought hit me like a slap in the face – could I be back in the old game – the one in which I am just a pawn on Johnny Walsh's chess board? The thought made me dizzy. I sank a couple of glasses of Spiced and smoked.

Later that day a friend of Ricky's moored his boat next to *Black Moon* – she still had the name *'Freedom'* painted on each side – and loaded a lot of diesel fuel onto my boat. He also brought a few gallons of water in big plastic barrels – I should be able to reach somewhere far away on the things he supplied. I paid cash – a lot of cash.

With my engine full, my water tanks full, my fridge and food stores full, I shook Ricky's hand and bade him a hearty farewell.

"Thanks for everything Ricky – you've probably saved my life – I owe you one"

Ricky laughed. "Think nothing of it man – you've brought a bit of excitement to the island –

makes a change from the general run of tourists all doing the same tings every day".

I hopped aboard. Ricky threw the mooring rope to me. "Stay out of trouble man – and send me a postcard when you get settled".

"Not sure I'm the settling type Ricky – but I will be in touch - and thanks again". With that I powered up the engine and slowly pulled away from the quay. We waved to each other for a while, then I went below as Ricky got in his van and drove back towards his house.

I guided the boat out into the main harbour area, set sail for the empty ocean. My first task was to make myself a strong cup of coffee and a ham sandwich. I sat in the small lounge enjoying my lunch – it was something 'normal' in my life – I had missed the routines of life over the past months – I was in need of some boring domesticity for a while. As I pulled out into the Caribbean I hoped I would be allowed to fulfil that need.

Chapter 27

I set a course towards Caracas – the capital of Venezuela – it took me 3 days of rough sailing and I was relieved to be back on land. I moored in the exclusive – and rather expensive – Playa Grande Yachting Club, situated approximately 12 miles from the city itself.

It was well appointed, filled with shiny modern super-yachts, glass and metal cruisers, power boats – my old vessel created a little interest from some of the younger members of the club who had not seen a craft built so strongly, using so much wood. *Black Moon* – or *Freedom* as she still pretended to be – was seen as a delightful antique to the modern sailor and I had a number of people asking me questions about the boat, about who I was, where I came from, where I was going and so on – exactly the sort of questions I did not want to be answering. Any one of these people could be in the pay of my enemies – there would be no way of knowing – Venezuela was not far from Barbados and they had been asking about me there – probably had this area covered by spies too. I gave rather vague replies and got out of the harbour as quickly as I could.

I had decided to leave my boat here for the time being as it was a known link to me. Boats are slow too – they are a leisure craft – not a quick form of travelling.

I took a local bus into the centre of Caracas, booked into a posh hotel under a false name – I had a second set of fake documents to back me up, made for me by an underworld contact in England some months earlier. I'd thought it might be necessary to make a run for it at some time – crime was an unpredictable business – and the police were not as stupid as people liked to believe. My documents stated that my name was Michael Shelton – I couldn't help being ironic about things – my occupation was stated as 'business owner'. The hotel accepted my ID and I was shown to my suite by a gangly youth who seemed to enjoy his work a little too much – maybe he was not all the ticket. He put my case and holdall down on the bed and I slipped him far too much money as a tip – maybe he had a reason for his uncontrolled grin after all.

I spent a couple of days relaxing, resting, making plans. The hot weather invigorated me. I spent enough time outdoors to get a slight tan. This would help me begin the transformation of my appearance which was to be an integral part of my strategy. I had decided to go back to England. Only there would I be able to get a clearer understanding of what was going on with my old enterprises – my old friends and acquaintances.

I had my fake ID – now I needed a new appearance to go with it. I started to let my hair and beard grow. I was in no hurry. I weighed my chances of finding out if anyone was still on my trail by staying put in my smart hotel suite for a few months – If nobody came knocking during that time, I could assume they had either lost my trail – given up their interest in me – or that I had eliminated the people who had been after me on that Caribbean island.

My boat would be safe in the overpriced marina – I paid up front for a year's mooring. I could collect her once I had assured myself it was safe to do so. I could travel faster without her – to be honest I had spent enough time at sea to keep my desire for 'life on the ocean wave' satisfied for a while.

After five and a half months of lazing about on the beach, drinking cocktails and overeating in posh restaurants, I decided I was brown enough to prevent being recognised. I dyed my hair and beard black and had gained almost a Stone in weight – I looked like a fat, scruffy Venezuelan in my ethnic clothing – purchased in local markets. With the addition of a pair of mirror shades and a dirty baseball cap, my own mother couldn't have picked me out of a police line-up. I had also developed a slight Venezuelan accent – partly by design – and added a few Spanish phrases to my speech. I would not have been considered anything but a local commoner. In fact the staff in the expensive restaurants I frequented began to give me unsavoury looks as I approached their tables. I was ready to put my plan into action.

My main goal was to sniff out any dodgy goings-on which might adversely effect me should I declare my true identity. I would decide on what action – if any – was necessary once I'd got a clearer picture of how things stood – both legally and safety-wise.

I also wanted to see if there was anyone behind Julio Montefiore's recent attempt to apprehend or eliminate me – was it just a personal grudge which had motivated him? – or was there someone higher up the food chain behind his actions.

I would need to speak to Mark Hopkins – had he been left alone when I abandoned my crime empire? What about Art Mercer – was the legitimate company – Black Moon Ltd still up and running?

I made arrangements to book out of the hotel which had been my home for almost half a year – I was a very different man to the one who had booked in!

I decided to leave in style, had a limousine collect me from the front foyer and drive me to the main airport. From there I took a scheduled flight to New York, where I spent a few days sightseeing and purchasing several items of clothing which would reinforce my new image.

From there I took another direct flight to Gatwick Airport. I had no trouble at all getting through customs. Michael Garvie was back in Blighty! Or rather, Michael Shelton was...

Chapter 28

It didn't take me long to find out the extent of the takeover of my erstwhile crime empire. It was total. I telephoned some of my main contacts – people who were surprised to discover that I was still alive. They informed me that the G10 set-up was still in operation – just with different management. Most of my contacts were in the same position as before – they answered to different bosses, that was all. Every one of the people I spoke to swore they did not know who was behind the takeover – they dealt with only middlemen – the exact same middlemen I had used when I was running the show.

I spoke to the middlemen. They swore they did not know who was behind the takeover – it was never disclosed to them. They got their instructions via phone calls and text messages – on unregistered mobiles, used solely for criminal activities.

So nobody knew nuffink – the old old story. I didn't buy it. I had the distinct impression that they were wary of speaking to me at all. A number of them attempted to get information from me regarding my whereabouts – no doubt there was a bounty on my head and they wanted to claim it if they could. I was glad that I had not gone to see any of them in person – my disguise was safe. It was my only advantage as things stood.

I called Art Mercer – who sounded genuinely pleased to hear from me. He had been concerned that I had suddenly disappeared off the face of the earth. Nobody involved in the crime business had contacted him – it seemed he was now out of the loop, free to run the legitimate company independently of outside control. I was pleased for him – I would happily trade places with him as things stood.

I had expected Black Moon Ltd to have acquired some new major shareholders soon after I left the country. However when I looked up the directors' list on the Companies House website, I was still, along with Art mercer, named as the major shareholder and director of the company. Maybe Art was telling the truth – I hoped so.

I still had no way of knowing who was ultimately behind the takeover of G10. Perhaps some government agency had been given the green light to smash my grip upon the many important influential people inside the military, press and political arenas. It made sense. I also had not ruled out the Italian mafia. I was beginning to doubt that it *was* them however, due to the fact that it had been Julio Montefiore himself who had tracked me down. It felt like a personal vendetta rather than an all out attack from the Cosa Nostra.

I was certain it was somebody who knew me well, behind the takeover. I could cross Paul Nixon and Johnny Walsh off my list, because they were both dead – which left Mark Hopkins, the man who had gone to extreme lengths to convince me that he was happy to settle down to a life of luxury in a country mansion and play 'Lord of the Manor'. I had accepted his words – hook, line and sinker – but

171

after what had happened I was not so sure. Mark Hopkins had been heavily involved in every bad thing that had happened to me in my coma dream – I wondered if these imaginings had in fact been warnings, omens, prophecies.

I hired a car, drove out to his home. After sitting around for several boring hours, I saw him come out of his front door and get into a brand new Bentley Continental Sport. I followed him onto the motorway and almost lost him as he accelerated into the distance – his car was much more powerful than mine. Luckily for me there was a lot of congestion further along the road and I caught up with him – at least until the bottleneck cleared.

The pace remained slow for about half an hour – we were heading south – possibly towards London – then the blockage cleared and Hopkins' car left me helpless in its wake. I turned off at the next junction, returned to his house. I was tempted to have a look through his windows but decided I didn't want to risk being spotted – if he was given a description of me, my disguise advantage would be gone. I gave up on the idea of following him about and went for a more direct approach. That evening I phoned him.

"Ahoy there Mark, how's tricks?"

"Who is this... Squirrel – is that you?"

"Might be"

"Where the hell have you been? – there's been all kinds of shit hitting all kinds of fans".

"Yeah, I know – that's why I decided to take a little holiday Mark – keeping my head down mate".

"Can't say I blame you – there have been a lot of heavy people asking questions about you. I told them I didn't know where you were – they eventually believed me".

"Any idea who these people were?"

"Julio Montefiore – the Mafia bloke – you know, the one who was arrested for the killing of Johnny Walsh and then released. He seemed to think you had something to do with it and was very angry about being set up – that was his view anyway – I have a sneaky feeling he was possibly correct in what he said – eh Mike?"

"I couldn't possibly comment".

"I would be surprised if you did".

"So how are things going with you now Mark – are things settling down – have you heard from Julio recently?"

"Not for about six months – he suddenly stopped bothering me – probably got fed up with me giving him the same answer over and over".

"Yes, I'm sure that's the reason" I couldn't help feeling a bit smug as I said this. It made the possibility that Montefiore had been working on his own behalf virtually conclusive – otherwise Mark would have had visits from other members of the Mafia.

"Why don't you pop over here Squirrel – it'd be nice to see you and I could put you in the picture regarding recent developments".

"Sounds a great idea Mark – are you still living in the same mansion or have you moved upmarket to a castle?"

"No, still the same hovel – do you know the address?"

"I think I may just about manage to find it Mark" I was feeling even more smug now. "How's Sunday suit you?"

"That'll be fine Michael – I'll be at church in the morning – but any time after about 1pm should be fine".

I wasn't sure at all that he wasn't taking the piss now – church? - I know he had professed to like the traditional lifestyle – but church? - surely he was having me on – I would find out soon enough.

"I'll say 1.30 then Mark – if that is OK with you"

"Perfect. I'll get the wife to keep Sunday lunch on hold until you get there".

I hung up in a fit of laughter – the guy was priceless. Either he thought I was the biggest idiot ever to roam the earth or he had changed beyond all recognition. Judging by his behaviour in my dreams it was probably the former.

I spent the interim period making certain arrangements and enquiries which brought me some surprising results. On Sunday I got up early, checked my equipment and drove slowly out to Mark's big house in the country. I parked my car where it was unlikely to be spotted and crept into his driveway – the big, wrought iron gates were not closed.

I kept behind a row of small trees and shrubbery which lined the drive, got down underneath a window. Most of the lights were off and as it was still twilight, I assumed that Mark and 'the Wife' were still asleep.

Last time I had visited Mark he lived alone – not so much as a dog to keep him company. I hoped he hadn't recently bought a couple of Rottweilers. I peered in through the window – into a cosy drawing room, done out like an Agatha Christie television show. Nobody there. I made my way to the next window – a study with a big imposing desk and a lot of filing cabinets.

During the next half hour I managed to get a peep into most of the downstairs rooms – kitchen, utility room, hallway – you name it, I saw into it – no-one around at this early hour. I had no way of looking into the upper windows – I was not Spiderman. I toured the lavish grounds, saw only two cars parked in the driveway – Mark's Bentley and a Volkswagen Golf convertible – which must belong to Mrs. Hopkins.

I was now satisfied that there were not a lot of armed men waiting to jump out the second I knocked on the front door. I would wait in the trees until Mark popped off to church and then have a sniff around inside.

Around 9am lights began to go on in some of the rooms – upstairs first, then the lower rooms. I caught a glimpse of a pretty blonde making breakfast in the kitchen – then later the Lord of the Manor appeared on a small balcony outside what must be the Master Bedroom. He was wearing a fancy silk dressing gown – I had to put my hand over my mouth to stifle a loud guffaw – it certainly looked like Mark was becoming a true country squire. I hoped so. I could do with someone on my side – or at least neutral. Mark knew enough of recent events to put me in the picture to some degree and I would make decisions regarding my future based on any useful information he would be able to furnish me.

My legs were starting to ache from crouching too long, so I moved to a new position behind a big tree – this gave me a wider view. I didn't smoke – the smell may alert Mark or Mrs Mark that there was an intruder in their grounds and I was beginning to feel just that – that I was intruding on a private and rather pleasant domestic arrangement – like a Peeping Tom. I pushed the feeling away – I had to protect myself until I knew what I was up against and if it meant a bit of covert observation – so be it.

Around 9.30 the front door opened, the Hopkins' got into the Bentley and Mark drove sedately down the gravel drive like he was in a Royal procession.

I wasted no time. I was inside the back door in a matter of minutes – courtesy of a skeleton key I had recently acquired as part of my special equipment. It took me ten minutes to check that there was nobody else in the building, a further fifteen to go through the papers in Mark's filing cabinets. I also found a wall-safe hidden behind a painting – how very quaint – but had neither the time, the skills or the equipment to open it. I found nothing incriminating – nothing which suggested that Mark Hopkins' conversion to Land-owner and Laird was anything other than genuine.

I carefully eliminated any signs that there had been an intruder in the house and made my way back to my car. I spent the next twenty minutes locating the local church and drove past slowly. Mark's Bentley was parked outside in the street – which was chock-a-block with churchgoers' vehicles.

I then drove back towards Mark's house, hid my car in a little wooded lane a few hundred yards from his driveway. Here I waited until I saw the Bentley return and park on the gravel drive. Mr. and Mrs. Hopkins were back from church.

I gave then half an hour to get settled and for Mrs. H. to get the Sunday roast started. Then I drove up his driveway, making the gravel fly about – I did not want to appear cautious – and slid to a halt rather too close to the Bentley' shiny paintwork.

Hearing me pull up, Mark came out to greet me – a big smile on his face – which faded when he saw some unknown 'Latino' standing in his driveway instead of his old mate Squirrel. My disguise had baffled him completely. He walked towards me – half cautious, half aggressive...

"Hey Gringo!" I shouted in my best Venezuelan accent, waving my hands about in an overdramatic style

"Who the hell are you?" he barked. I moved towards him like an overexcited puppy.

"Don't you recognise your old pal?" I asked – bounding closer. He took a step back and looked at me, intently puzzled.

"Can't say I do mate – who are you?" - and then it dawned on him like the sun coming over the horizon. "Squirrel! - is that you mate? Fuck me – you've changed a bit!" I started to laugh out loud – Mark joined in.

"I got you there mate – the look on your face was priceless". We shook hands, stood beaming and laughing – Mark did most of the beaming – I did most of the laughing.

"Come inside and meet the Missus – you'll like her, she's got a sick sense of humour too".

"She's need one to marry you Mark!" I quipped.

"You may have a point there" he replied. We walked into the foyer – I pretended to be impressed – even though I had been there not so long ago. He showed me around the house with pride – it was a very nice place and his taste was exquisite – as was his wife who was busy in the large kitchen, currently tipping a boiling saucepan of potatoes into a large colander over the fancy Boston-style sink.

"This is Jacquie – the current Mrs. Hopkins".

"Mark's favourite old joke" said Jacquie, laughing - "Pleased to meet you Michael – my husband has told me a lot about you – I'm sure most of it is bullshit – but it's nice to put a face to the legend at last – although I must say you look a lot different to how I had you pictured in my head".

"He looks a lot different to how I had him pictured in my head too!" Mark said. We all laughed – although Jacquie was mainly being polite – not yet being in on the joke.

I shook hands with Mrs. Hopkins and felt a pang of jealousy – she was a real little cracker – as the saying used to go in my day – very blonde, slim but with enough curves to elicit a certain amount of interest from any man. She had a highly intelligent look in her eyes and a friendly, amused persona. Mark was punching well above his weight! I guess a Bentley and a big country house have their attractions too, I told myself. That was a bit mean of me but envy is a bad companion.

I followed Mark back into the lounge where he offered me a drink.

"Still on the rum Squirrel?" he asked, opening a very well stocked drinks cabinet.

"Yep, sure am – got any Captain Morgan's Spiced?"

"No, sorry mate – I only have quality booze these days – how about a Kraken?"

"Sounds reasonable" I replied. Kraken rum was top quality and a lot smoother than my usual brand – it was also a lot more expensive.

He poured the drinks – both Krakens – we sat in a couple of adjacent armchairs sipping our drinks and observing each other in silence.

Mark looked a bit fatter and a lot happier. His eyes held the friendly twinkle of a man who was more than content with his lot in life. If he was still involved in any dark dealings – let alone being behind the takeover of G10 – I'd not only eat my hat but I'd vomit it back up and eat it again with a spoon!

The sound of a dinner gong! I couldn't help but laugh. Mark smiled, half amused, half proud of the gong.

"We like to do things properly in this house" he said.

"I can see that" I replied as we walked into the large, very formal dining room – double doors, large shiny table covered with Indian Cotton table cloth – all the best crystal glasses and highly polished cutlery. It was impressive.

Jacquie had the plates warming in a serving trolley – the vegetables were in fancy dishes, covered by silver domed lids. It was like dining with royalty. The food itself – roast beef – which Mark – as head of the family – carved beautifully – carrots, sprouts, parsnips, cauliflower cheese, Yorkshires, roasties – all cooked to perfection and served by the exquisite Mrs Hopkins, who smelled as good as she looked. I could see why Mark was happy to settle down – I wouldn't mind a bit of this good living myself.

"For what we are about to receive, may the Lord make us truly thankful" - Mark said Grace before we tucked into the feast. It was textbook. I was impressed.

"Amen" said Mrs. Hopkins – I half mumbled something – feeling embarrassed – a bit out of my depth in this squeaky clean, highly traditional setting.

We ate our food with only minimal, polite, conversation. The grub tasted out of this world – I was starting to wonder if I was back in some sort of euphoric coma dream – but it was real. Mark had created the perfect upper class conservative lifestyle – every detail perfect. He seemed to genuinely love it. I envied him now but was pleased that he had made the perfect life for himself.

After pudding – home made sherry trifle - and coffee, I accompanied Mark into the lounge where he offered me a very expensive cigar and a five star brandy in a massive balloon glass. Jacquie – the perfect trad wife - was in the kitchen loading the top-of-the-range dishwasher.

We sat in green Chesterfield armchairs like a couple of inmates of a very exclusive Gentlemen's club – I couldn't help grinning – this was great fun. Mark looked proudly on – he had every right to be proud. Top Notch.

"Well Squirrel – maybe you would like to tell me why you have decided to visit me so suddenly – and in a heavy disguise?" He grinned his boyish grin.

"I suppose I should really – after such a nice welcome." I took a long pull on my cigar. "I have been out of the country for quite a while – had a bit of trouble as you may know".

"Of course I know – had some hassle myself for a while".

"After the assassination of Paul Nixon and the overnight takeover of G10 I thought it wise to keep a low profile for a while". I sipped my brandy. "Anyway to cut a long story short, I ended up in Venezuela after a bit of a shoot-out in the Caribbean".

"Nothing very exciting then?" Mark Joked. I shrugged.

"No – just the normal everyday activity – being hunted by the Mafia, that sort of thing." I gave Mark a concise rundown of the last few months events.

"Sounds exciting" he said with a grimace which indicated he was glad it was me, not him, who had experienced those events.

"The novelty wears off quickly I can assure you". We both laughed.

"So what are you going to do next Squirrel?"

"Not sure – I wanted to speak to a few old friends and acquaintances – see if I could get a clearer picture of how things might stand if I came back to England".

"I've not really heard much to be honest mate – not since all the trouble with your pal Nixon – and Johnny Walsh being killed. Had a couple of coppers, some dodgy Italians and a man who said he was Secret Service round here asking questions – but that was a while ago – I've not been visited since. I'm out of the game mate – as you can see – settled down you might say".

"A very nice setup you have got too mate – can't say I'm not a little envious. You got out just in time."

"That's true – I've been very lucky".

We spent another hour chatting about old times and life in general – then I told Mark I had to get going and we agreed I would visit again when next I was in the area. We shook hands and Mrs. Hopkins kissed me on the cheek – she smelled very nice – I drove off feeling angry for some reason.

My visit to Mark Hopkins' place had been enjoyable but ultimately unrewarding. I was no nearer to finding out whether it was safe for me to be in the country or not. Mark now knew of my disguise, so I would soon find out if he was trustworthy or not. If a posse of bad men appeared on the horizon all of a sudden, I would know the information had come from him. Nobody else knew about my changed appearance – Mark was the only one who had seen me – I had telephoned all my other contacts. I didn't expect that to happen. Mark had convinced me he was out of the picture for good – living his happy life with his happy wife.

I booked into a small hotel on the outskirts of Southampton – I wanted to check out a couple of things before deciding how to play it moving forward.

The first person I wanted to see was Kirsty, my sister. I drove over to her house early next morning but she was not in. I decided to come back later. In the meantime I went into Southampton to buy a few items – including black hair dye – I wanted to keep my disguise in place a while longer. The town was busy – I was forced to take refuge in a pub for half an hour but managed to come through my shopping trip virtually unscathed.

When I got back to Kirsty's house, there was a light on in the front room. I wondered how surprised my sister would be when she answered the door and saw me in all my Venezuelan glory. As it turned out it was I who was surprised. Kirsty didn't answer the door. Johnny Walsh did. He was holding an automatic pistol and smiling like a Cheshire cat.

Chapter 29

"Ahoy there Shipmate! Long time no see". I just stood there, in shock, looking blank. It seemed an appropriate response. He waved the gun about, beckoning me to go inside Kirsty's house. I complied.

"Where's my sister?" I stammered.

"Oh, don't worry Mike, I've taken care of her!" he said.

"When you say 'taken care of' – what are you saying. He laughed out loud at my concern.

"Don't worry Mike, she's still alive and well – she moved to a bigger house a couple of months ago – I bought this house off her – thought it might be the best place for me to sit it out while I waited for you to return to your old stomping grounds – you did a good job of escaping my clutches – to be honest I was impressed by how you kept below the radar for so long – I've had men out all over the globe looking for you – but to no avail".

"Sorry if I caused you any inconvenience". I quipped.

"To be honest, you did cause me a little bit of trouble when I found out you were planning to have me killed".

"It was nothing personal Johnny – you were getting in too deep with the Italians – I found out you had plans to undermine me – just business" I tried to sound confident but I wasn't even fooling myself. I was motioned into the sitting room – the

184

décor was the same as the last time I had been here – when my sister lived here.

"Take a seat Mike" Johnny barked. He was not smiling – he looked quite angry, now that the introductory niceties had been completed. I sat down on Kirsty's sofa.

"What have you done with my sister?" I asked. Johnny Walsh laughed – there was no humour in his laugh.

"I have to thank you for giving me the idea – in fact you have been giving me a lot of ideas. You seem to be making your life merge with that dream you told me about – when you were unconscious in hospital. Arranging to have my head blown off and planting the weapon on Julio – that was classic. Unfortunately for you I knew about the plan in advance – your pal Nixon was working both sides of the equation you might say – a sort of self-made double agent – fingers in everybody's pies. The only difference was that I caught on to his little act and had him taken care of – you believed every line he fed you – but you always were very naïve Mike".

I was shocked at this revelation. Paul Nixon – my most trusted colleague, a traitor, a spy, a fraud. I had come to trust him completely and all the time he had been getting paid by both sides. He'd arranged to have Walsh eliminated and at the same time planned with Walsh to create a fake murder – just like the one I had dreamt up while comatose.

It was clear to me now that Johnny was fully aware of what I was up to – I on the other hand did not know that Johnny had been one step ahead of me all the way down the line – thanks to Paul Nixon.

Johnny got rid of Paul after his murder had been faked – he was too dangerous to be kept running loose. That left Johnny and his Mafia pals free and clear to takeover the entire G10 organisation, which they had accomplished in a matter of days – they had all of Paul Nixon's files, so gained control of the media sources, the police and government organisations they needed in order to portray the murder of Johnny Walsh as genuine and gloss over the killing of Paul Nixon.

As Johnny talked, I learned that Julio Montefiore had felt a personal grievance against me and, no doubt egged on by Walsh – had tracked me down in an attempt to regain his lost pride by killing me personally. Unfortunately that little plan hadn't worked out too well for him.

"What have you done with my sister?" I repeated. He had avoided answering me before – instead giving me a rambling dissertation upon how clever he had been and how he now controlled G10 – with the Italians mainly controlling the cash generating end of the business. Johnny was top dog regarding the manipulation of powerful individuals, companies, organisations and governments – my old role you might say.

"Don't worry about your sister, Mike – like I said, she's moved out – some friends of mine are looking after her welfare – for the moment"

"You mean you've had her kidnapped?"

"You put the idea into my head Mike".

"So what is it you want me to do – after all you wouldn't need to put pressure on me by grabbing Kirsty if you just wanted to kill me?".

"You're still a bright boy Mike"

"I do my best to keep up".

The next hour was filled with Johnny Walsh giving me instructions. I knew exactly what he wanted me to do – and it would not include survival.

Chapter 30

I cast off, steered the *Black Moon* out of the harbour. The burble of the powerful diesel engine shattered midnight silence. It was just after 1am and I was at the beginning of a long journey which would end in death. My death.

Johnny Walsh had set the parameters of my remaining existence. I had exactly 21 days – three weeks – to live. If I arrived late at my destination, Johnny would kill my sister. If I arrived on time, I would die. Along with a lot of Italians.

There was a big Mafia meeting arranged. All the top names would be there. Johnny wanted them gone. This would set him free of all restraint, give him total control of G10 and the entire Crime Syndicate. He would have the western world in his pocket.

His plan was simple – and entirely based upon what I had told him about the nightmares I had experienced whilst in a coma. It was ironic to say the least. Even the chosen method of destroying his enemies was taken directly from my dreams. It was twisted.

I was to sail my boat into Naples Bay, moor up next to a hotel jetty. A very expensive hotel, filled with wealthy powerful guests – including several Mafia Dons. Johnny himself had called the meeting – had offered the possibility of handing over the whole G10 blackmail operation to the Italians and it was too big a prize for them to refuse. They would all be there – fruitlessly waiting for Johnny to turn up and give them ultimate power over the British establishment – and more.

I would slip my little boat in among the huge super-yachts and wait until I got the word from Johnny that all of his intended victims were in position. Then I would press a button and the world would end. For me. For everyone in the hotel. For anyone within a two mile radius in fact. Later, for perhaps thousands of people. Nuclear bombs can do that.

During my visit to England, Johnny had arranged for some Special Forces soldiers – controlled through G10 – to plant a small atomic device deep in the keel space of my boat. It could be operated either by remote wireless signal, which Johnny Walsh had – or by the pressing of an outrageously large red button on the side of the bomb's casing. I was to press this button. Johnny had lost none of his sense of humour – the button had a sign above it saying 'Do Not Press' in large red capital letters. The comic effect was lost on me. It was sinister.

I would be instructed to press this button at a certain time. If I refused, my sister would be killed and Johnny would set off the bomb himself by remote control. It was a no win situation for me. I also felt that my sister's chances of ultimate survival were pretty slim even if I did do what I was told. Why would Johnny keep Kirsty alive as a witness? – he had never kept any other threats to his dominance around for long – this would be no different. I had no illusions that ultimately my sister was doomed.

I also felt it would be incredibly evil on my part to sacrifice hundreds of people just to keep one woman alive – regardless of who she was. I had three weeks to come up with a plan to thwart Johnny Walsh once and for all. He would not suspect that I would be willing to sacrifice my sister if necessary – he believed the dream too much – wanted everything to happen like it did before. He was quite, quite mad.

I had the cards stacked in my favour. If only I could work out how to play them. I could abandon my boat – and the bomb - in the middle of the North Atlantic. I still had my dinghy on board. It could get me to some silent, secret cove from where I could disappear forever.

But Johnny would come after me – and would eventually find me. He had the global reach and resources. Also my sister would be dead. I might be willing to sacrifice her if there was no other choice – but I would be damned if I would do so under lesser circumstances. So I had to finish Johnny – once and for all. I had to destroy G10 – completely and utterly. And I had nobody I could rely upon but myself. Nuclear shit or bust.

Chapter 31

One option I had not considered until now – after my sense of desperation had increased with every nautical mile I moved closer to the endgame, was to blow the bomb – and myself – to smithereens while still a long way out to sea. This would thwart Walsh's plan, make his continued holding of my sister as a hostage pointless. However, knowing Johnny Walsh as I did , I thought it likely he would kill Kirsty out of spite.

I thought about contacting some police force or other – what country would I go to? – and what was the likelihood that they had not been infiltrated by G10 at some level? Chances were that nothing positive would be achieved.

I was convinced that Johnny would kill my sister before long – she may be dead already. I had decided not to let her safety be my primary consideration – it would simply limit my options with no increase in the likelihood of her release whatever. She would have to take her chances, hope that fate was smiling on her when the shit hit the fan – which it was soon going to do.

Taking these thoughts to their logical conclusion and weighing the risks in the balance I suddenly had a breakthrough – in logic at least. If I was not going to make my sister's safety my number one concern - then what was it to be? To stop Johnny Walsh from blowing up some Mafia people – and a lot of innocent strangers? It was a compelling argument. There was one other, even more compelling outcome I wished to bring about – my own personal survival. How did that weigh against the lives of others?

I began to consider the idea of simply disembarking from *Black Moon*, keeping her stationary in the middle of the vast ocean – using my dinghy to get to a place of safety. It would be some time before Johnny would become aware of my disappearance, that his bomb was not going to be delivered. He had gambled on my desire to save my sister as an infallible control lever. He had been wrong. I was as surprised about this as he would soon be. It was my Ace in the Hole.

If I went one step further and contacted as many police and military organisations – in several countries – and maybe the press – surely somebody would be forced to do something to prevent the bombing? Surely G10 didn't have ultimate control of everything? There was a good chance I could make enough of a stink to force some action.

My only concern was that my boat was being tracked. Johnny may be monitoring the position of the craft continually - have hidden cameras on board so he could make sure I was still present on the boat.

I could counteract the first problem by keeping the boat moving towards its intended destination – only slow the speed. This would be noticed, but there was not a lot he could do about it and he would probably deduce that the slow pace - initially at least – was temporary – I would remain within allocated time parameters for a day or two.

As long as I was still on schedule – or not far behind it – Johnny would probably let things slide. By the time he did something about it I would have made my contacts and escaped. It was then up to the gods as to the final outcome – let the dice fall where they may.

I decided this was my best option – I turned the boat towards the African coast. I had, after all come via a stopover in Africa on my way to Venezuela – so it should not seem too strange if I stopped there on my way back – maybe I needed fuel or rations - or had a minor repair that I deemed necessary. It would certainly not look too odd – that's for sure.

I could then get to landfall in my dinghy – after pointing my boat out into the middle of the North Atlantic - and take shelter in some quiet African cove. I would not risk actually mooring as it was possible there would be G10 people acting as look-outs in many of the ports. There had been before – so it was almost certain to be so again.

The fact that I had been moving towards a port, then turned around and carried on without reaching it, would almost certainly be understood as my having solved whatever little problem I'd had, by my own actions – thereby no longer needing to dock. I thought it sounded logical enough for Johnny to interpret my actions along these lines – if not, well so be it!

It took me a day and a half to get close enough to the African continent to risk using the dinghy. It had a small outboard engine with a range of only a hundred miles or so.

If I miscalculated, I would run out of fuel, become stranded at sea. Not a pleasant thought.

The coastal reefs were dangerous around here - as many larger boats had found to their eternal regret.

I lowered the rubber boat into the ocean – which thankfully was fairly calm at the moment. It was attached to the *Black Moon* by a rope. I then turned my beautiful Westsail 32 around and set her on a slow course to nowhere. I felt emotional, letting her go to her destruction like this but I could think of no better option.

"Goodbye old girl – the best of luck! Hope to see you again one day". I jumped down into my dinghy, sat there watching my lovely boat sail away to oblivion. It was heartbreaking.

I started the outboard motor, pointed the dinghy towards where I estimated land to be. By my calculations I was approximately 50 nautical miles from the coast of Senegal. I hoped to land fairly close to Dakar. I knew there would be modern facilities in this busy tourist spot – and plenty of telephones from which to call the authorities – as many of them as possible.

It was late afternoon when I saw a spit of white sand up ahead and knew I was now approaching the coast. The reefs were causing a lot of nasty underwater currents and my control of the little craft had lessened. It was beginning to bounce around like a bingo ball. I hung on to the tiller in an attempt to control the direction. I had spotted a little bay – flatter water – off to starboard. I forced the tiller hard and the boat twisted on its axis. The backwash from the waves rocked the boat viciously and I grabbed a rope to stop myself being thrown overboard. It took a further ten minutes of unpleasant buffeting before I reached calmer water, made my way directly toward the beach.

As I got closer I saw – further to starboard – a small harbour. I would not land there. I thought it would be a good idea to get fairly close though, then sink my boat and swim in.

The port would offer facilities like communications and transport. I needed to get lost in Dakar as quickly as possible.

I got within a quarter mile of the little jetty, then jumped into the water. I struggled to tip the boat far enough for her to fill. Eventually the grey rubber craft began to take on water, get low in the ocean and finally with a mass of gurgling bubbles, disappear down towards Davy Jones' Locker.

I swam towards land. It was hard going but I had known worse and made it safely onto the sand about half a mile to the left of the harbour. I let myself dry off in the hot sun, checked I still had my passport and money – all safely packed in a plastic zip-up bag – and straightened my clothing, before walking casually towards the jetty.

Port de Joal Fadiouth was situated approximately 80 miles from Dakar. There were plenty of taxis to be had and the facilities in this area were modern.

I booked into the Auberge le Djembé – a basic beach-front three-star hotel with all the facilities I needed and few guests. There was a pool, a bar and a small restaurant. I booked in as Mr. Shelton.

In the morning I took the small hotel shuttle bus direct to the airport, got a flight to Paris. From there I took an overnight train to Calais, then a hovercraft to Portsmouth, England.

I spent the night in a cheap hotel before hiring a Transit van and driving the short distance to Southampton. I parked up outside my sister's house, the last place I had seen Johnny Walsh.

It was around noon that I saw movement – the front door opened and Johnny himself came out, carrying a briefcase. He looked like a stockbroker on his way to the city – smart pinstripe suit, heavy overcoat – unbuttoned. I was surprised to say the least. Johnny did not usually dress in this formal manner – I could only assume that it was some sort of disguise – which might indicate that he was off on a mission of some sort – rather than just popping down to the local shop to buy milk.

I was faced with a dilemma. My plan had been to find Johnny, force him to release my sister. I could still do this but wanted to have a snoop around the house first. If I let him disappear now I might never find him again. On the other hand he may be back in half an hour with his weekly shopping.

In the end I decided to kill two birds with one stone. I jumped out of the van and casually walked towards him. He was not looking at me but glancing at his watch. I sprung forward – bringing a revolver out of my pocket as I did so.

"Ahoy shipmate – no sudden moves - or I'll blow your fucking brains out right here and now!" He spun round, saw me – a look of fright and surprise flashed across his face – he had obviously not expected a visit from me.

"Mike!" he stuttered "What are you doing here? I thought you were sailing the ocean's blue".

"Guess again Scumbag!" I snarled. "Back inside – now!" He turned, began walking back towards the house. "If anything I don't like happens when we get inside – such as any of your minions making an appearance or any attempt to grab a weapon, you will not live to see the consequences – is that clear?"

"Crystal" he replied.

He unlocked the front door and we entered. I made him lock the door from the inside and give me the key, which he did. I then made him walk through the house – there was nobody there. Finally I made sure the back door was locked and took possession of that key also.

"OK then Johnny – me old mucker – first I'd like you to tell me where my sister Kirsty is". I waved my gun in his face just to emphasise the importance of a positive answer to my question. He laughed.

"You really are making a mountain out of a molehill Michael – she's absolutely fine I can assure you".

"I asked you where she was Pal – don't piss me about".

"What are you going to do if I refuse to answer? – if I'm dead you'll never see her alive again". He had a point and we both knew it.

What he didn't know though, was the fact that I had come to terms with the likely death of my sister – he had less power here than he thought he had. I shot him in the arm. He screeched and jumped away from me. Blood gushed from his left arm. A look of shock on his face competed with a look of pain. I had unsettled him. He knew I wasn't pissing about – no longer could he make Michael Garvie jump to his twisted tune. I was top dog now and he was quickly realising it.

"OK OK, for fuck's sake Michael, calm down!" I shot him in the right arm.

"Don't fucking tell me to calm down you piece of shit – just answer my fucking question – where the fuck is my sister Kirsty?".

"She's safe – I promise, she's not even kidnapped – I was bullshitting you – like in your dream – you told me about how you were made to do stuff by some bad guys who had your sister held hostage – I just said it to see if I could make you do stuff too – that's it – no bomb – no kidnap – just a stupid joke – honest!" I raised the gun and pointed it right in his terrified face.

"You've gotta be fucking kidding me".

"I'm not – I just bought her house off her – that's why I'm here – I knew you'd appear sooner or later and I wanted to give you some shit for the way you planned to have me killed by Paul Nixon." He looked scared – and he had every right to be now that I was in total control of his continued existence. Part of me believed him. Part of me didn't.

What he said was logical – and given his naturally twisted sense of humour – and revenge – it was plausible.

"So, for the final time – where the fuck is my sister – you've got ten seconds... 9...8..."

"She's living just five minutes from here – Gordon Avenue – number 112 – its a nicer area – you must know it". I did in fact know Gordon Avenue – the houses there were all four bed detached or larger.

"She could not afford to live in Gordon Avenue".

"She can – she's got a good paying job now – she works for me – on the legal side of things – I've been helping her".

"And why would you do that Johnny?"

"I always liked your sister – she's never done me any harm – I wanted to balance the equation – if I was doing you harm I might as well do her some good – I know it sounds crazy but it made sense to me Mike".

"Bullshit" I snapped. He flinched – maybe thought I was going to finish him off there and then. "I think it a lot more likely you thought it would be fun to gain control of Kirsty in some way – make her reliant upon you for her livelihood – one more way of getting back at me maybe?"

"You really have become a cynical bastard haven't you Garvie?" he showed genuine anger as he spoke – which could be a sign that he actually meant what he said about helping Kirsty – he was always a little taken by my sister's charms when we were teens – perhaps he wanted to comfort her after my planned demise.

"If I have, then you are one of the main reasons for it". It sounded sulky – it was sulky. I was not comfortable getting into relationship complications.

"I'm going to tie you up now Johnny – maybe when I come back – or if I come back – from checking that Kirsty is alright – I will phone for a doctor – you could probably do with one" I sneered.

"You don't need to tie me up – both my arms are fucked – I'm losing a lot of blood".

"All the more reason you'd better hope I come back in one piece – because if I don't, your chances will be slim".

I grabbed some old marine rope from a cupboard in what had been my sister's spare room and tied Walsh's damaged and bleeding arms behind his back, securely attached to a large metal radiator below the window. I also tied his legs – tight – he protested but I was no longer a soft touch. He looked alarmed and crestfallen – like a trussed up turkey waiting for Christmas – it was pathetic – and quite hilarious.

"Be a good boy and I'll be back in ten minutes". I blew him a kiss and stormed out of the house. It took me two minutes to drive to 112 Gordon Avenue.

Kirsty screamed when she saw me looming towards her as she opened the front door. I had forgotten that my Venezuelan disguise was still in place.

"Relax sis – it's me Mike – your long-lost brother". She stopped screaming. We went inside. The hallway was quite large – the house was well-appointed – definitely a marked improvement on her little terraced home.

"You fucking dick!" she shouted, hitting me on the arm. "You scared the shit out of me. What the hell are you doing dressed up like that?".

"It's a long story"

"It always is with you".

I spent ten minutes giving her a highly condensed version of recent events. She rolled her eyes.

"When are you going to settle down and face reality Mike?" - she laughed as she asked me this question. Kirsty was not judgemental – just exasperated.

"You know me Sis – never grew up, that's my problem".

"You said it pal".

"So how long you been living at the posh end of town? Did you win the pools or something?".

"No, of course not – don't even do the pools. I just got a better job – from an old friend of yours in fact – Johnny Walsh".

"Oh yeah, how is Johnny these days?".

"He's living in my old house – weird but true. Bought it off me cash – and gave me a really good job in his company too. Personal Assistant. Which is another name for a glorified dogsbody – but to be honest it's money for old rope – couldn't be better. He's been a big help to me since you disappeared off the face of the earth again".

"I must stop doing that" I quipped.

"That'll be the day Mike". We both smiled, rather strained smiles. I could see that my behaviour had caused my sister some considerable stress and anxiety of late. I hadn't finished with her yet.

"So Johnny has been good to you, helping you out and suchlike, eh?"

"He's been a tower of strength – I don't know how I would have managed without him to tell the truth".

"And he hasn't tried to kidnap you or threaten you in any way then?"

"Of course not! What the hell has happened to you Mike? I swear you've gone completely bonkers this time – you really ought to get some help. Seriously Mike". I shrugged.

"Listen Sis, I've had a few complications to deal with lately. I won't bore you with the full details but I might just be able to get it sorted once and for all – just a few more loose ends to tidy up".

"I'll look forward to that day". I gave her a hug – she pretend punched my arm. I began moving back towards the hallway.

"Look Sis, there's just one more thing I want you to do"

"What?"

"I want you to wait half an hour and then go to your old house – Johnny's new house – and bring a doctor with you".

"A doctor? What the heck are you up to Mike? Don't do anything stupid".

"I've already done it. Me and Johnny had a slight misunderstanding – I got the wrong end of the stick about something. He's been shot". I legged it out of the house, got in my car and drove back to Johnny Walsh's house. He was still at home.

"Johnny – I've been to see Kirsty – it seems you were telling the truth and you've been helping her".

"I did tell you"

"Yeah but you've told me a lot of things lately – like you were going to kill her and there was a nuclear bomb on my boat".

"Yeah, sorry about that. You pissed me off when you tried to kill me – I've always been rather sensitive to that kind of thing".

"So how come you were not killed then? Who was it that got his head blown off? How did you find out about the attempt on your life?"

"That's a lot of questions – I'll tell you what I know. I first found out that you – and specifically Paul Nixon – had taken a contract out on me. I got the information from the killer himself – he was a Scot from Edinburgh – Gordon McKlintock – I had used his services myself – he was a reliable ally – to me that is"

"Go on".

"Although he worked for the Mafia and Paul Nixon from time to time, he was freelance. He decided to warn me – in fact he arranged another victim – an old enemy of his – brought him tied up, in a van and forced him to dress in some of my clothes. He then did the deed and waited until Julio Montefiore turned up for the meeting I had arranged with him – he planted the gun in his car as per your instructions and that was mission accomplished – you know the rest of what happened."

"How come the police didn't let on that you were not the actual victim – they must have known?"

"We made sure the killing was investigated by cops we had in our pocket, through G10 – they said what we told them to say – it was not a problem convincing everyone that I was really dead – even Paul Nixon believed it – until I appeared one night and blew him away that is. He was very surprised to see me I can tell you".

"I'll bet he was!"

"I guess Paul Nixon and Julio Montefiore had us both jumping through their little hoops for a time".

"Neither of us was as clever as he thought he was, as it turned out". I laughed out loud.

"What's tickling you Mike?"

"I just thought about how you really had me jumping through a few hoops of your own – I even abandoned my fucking boat in the middle of the North Atlantic – she's still out there somewhere – unless she's been stolen – or sunk".

"Like I said, I was angry that you tried to have me killed – though I expect you had been slowly pushed in that direction by Paul Nixon. I was getting similar manipulation from Julio".

"Well *he* won't be bothering you again – that I can promise you".

"That's nice to know". Johnny said.

"In fact, as far as I can see it – there is no longer a threat from the Mafia – if Julio was behind all the threats and killings. The Dons have taken over the G10 organisation – they probably don't want to drag us into it. The fallout from what we could tell the authorities – names and positions of their controlled assets in government, media, big business, the military – and so on – it could blow their entire operation".

"I think we are in the clear" replied Johnny. "Those Italians have alibis coming out of their pores. They have enough control over the police to ensure that they will never be prosecuted. They also think that there are procedures in place - that the authorities will be alerted if I suddenly disappear – I have a system to cover my own ass too".

"I wish I'd thought of that".

"Don't worry Mike – I've covered you too – it was only Julio who wanted you dead. The big wigs in Naples find the whole thing amusing – they respect what you were able to achieve with G10 – highly impressed in fact".

"Especially now that they have stolen the entire fucking organisation from me!" I laughed.

"Any chance of you phoning an ambulance mate - I'm feeling a little peaky?"

"Taken care of Mate, already taken care of"

Chapter 32

Johnny had a few awkward questions to answer when he got out of hospital. The local police were not impressed with his answers regarding an unknown intruder having shot him and then run off, never to be seen again and leaving no trace – but they had to accept it – there was no evidence to the contrary.

I spent that time tracking down my boat. *Black Moon* had been taken into custody by the Senegalese Customs, just hours after I had set her loose in the North Atlantic. She had been kept in a police dock ever since. The authorities had traced her to Dakar, where she had been previously and they had a description of the man who had been seen piloting her.

They had also found out that her name had been changed – that '*Freedom*' was not her legal moniker. It took a lot of explaining – and a few hundred dollars – to get them to allow me to take her into my own custody.

I wasted no time getting out to sea – I feared they may decide to go back on the deal. As it turned out, I made good progress, suffered no official interference.

As soon as I got back to Dover – with her original name restored, I moored up in the same dock which had been the centre of so many incidents over the past few years. It felt good to be back.

There was now a real chance for normality to take root in my life. I really hoped so. I was tired of all the activity. The brain damage which had addicted me to danger seemed to have reset itself. I no longer wanted anything interesting to happen for the rest of my life.

It took two months to cut all links to my murky past. Art Mercer was no longer involved in any illegal activity – neither was Mark Hopkins.

Johnny Walsh had now also moved well clear of anything dodgy – he made sure the Mafia had full control – and responsibility for – all of his previous operations. It was thanks to him that they promised to forget me and all that had happened recently. It would not be good business on their part to let bad feelings drag on. They were after all was said and done, a commercial operation, concerned with profit margins.

Now it was my turn to move on. I sold all my shares in my legal and illegal companies. I cashed in all my assets and moved to a nice little cottage in Norfolk – a long way from anyone I knew.

It was on the river Yare – not far from the small village of Bramerton, with a local shop and a small marina where I could get my boat fixed and maintained when required.

The *Black Moon* looked large and rather magnificent sitting among the reeds and willow trees which lined the river here. It was lovely.

A couple of months later I got an invitation through the post to attend the wedding of Kirsty Garvie and Johnny Walsh. I sent back the RSVP saying that I would not be able to attend but wished them the very best of luck. I said I'd visit once I'd got fully settled.

I had a house to decorate and a garden to dig. I spent the day doing just those things. Then I went in for a well-earned rest and some food. I took my time eating the ham sandwich – savouring every mouthful. It tasted wonderful. Then an early night with a good book and a glass of Captain Morgan's Spiced rum. I slept well and rose early. I opened the curtains. The sun shone in on my brand new life.

"Ahoy World!" I said, with a smile. The world smiled back.

The End

Printed in Great Britain
by Amazon